Join the dedicated team
in St. Stephen's Emergency Department,
where the pace is hectic, tempers flare
and sexual tension is in the air!

In *A Wife for Dr. Cunningham*,
junior doctor Hannah Blake and
Dr. Robert Cunningham can't stop striking sparks
off one another. But will they take their fiery
relationship beyond the emergency room?

And don't miss
Dr. Mathieson's Daughter
by Maggie Kingsley
Coming soon in Medical Romance!™

Dear Reader,

I've always thought working in an emergency department must be one of the most exciting, terrifying and challenging jobs in the world. When my own mother was whisked into an emergency unit recently, I found myself wondering what motivated the people who work there. They'd have to be very special people of course—knowing every day could bring life-threatening situations—but surely these people must also be like you and me, with their own fears, hopes and dreams? These thoughts inspired me to create Robert Cunningham and Hannah Blake, and I do hope you enjoy reading about them in *A Wife for Dr. Cunningham,* as much as I enjoyed telling their story.

And as for the next book in the EMERGENCY DOCTOR'S DUO, *Dr. Mathieson's Daughter?* Well, I couldn't possibly leave blond-haired, blue-eyed Elliot Mathieson with no one in his life, now could I? So I thought he should find happiness, too, but not in a way he could ever have imagined! Coming soon!

Maggie Kingsley

A Wife for Dr. Cunningham

Maggie Kingsley

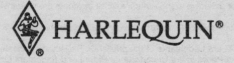

HARLEQUIN®

TORONTO • NEW YORK • LONDON
AMSTERDAM • PARIS • SYDNEY • HAMBURG
STOCKHOLM • ATHENS • TOKYO • MILAN • MADRID
PRAGUE • WARSAW • BUDAPEST • AUCKLAND

ISBN 0-373-06313-X

A WIFE FOR DR. CUNNINGHAM

First North American Publication 2001

Copyright © 2001 by Maggie Kingsley

This edition published by arrangement with Harlequin Books S.A.

Visit us at www.eHarlequin.com

Printed in U.S.A.

CHAPTER ONE

DR ROBERT CUNNINGHAM groaned as he stared down at the file on his desk, the file with its neatly typed label proclaiming that Dr Hannah Blake had been appointed to St Stephen's Accident and Emergency Unit as its newest member of staff.

He didn't need this, not right now. Right now what he needed was sleep—hour upon hour of dreamless sleep—not some junior doctor straight out of med school, hanging onto his coat tails wanting guidance and advice.

If he'd only had his wits about him he would have attempted to persuade Mr Mackay, the consultant in charge of A and E, to allow Elliot to take care of this Hannah Blake. Taking care of women was the blond-haired, blue-eyed SHO's speciality, whereas he—

Don't think, his mind warned. Don't remember. Quickly he pushed the file to one side and reached for his morning mail, only to discover it was the usual boring collection of advertising circulars and bumph. The usual uninspiring selection sent to every special registrar in the country—except for the catalogue at the bottom. The catalogue addressed to Dr Laura Cunningham.

Sudden tears filled his eyes as he gazed down at it.

A year.

It was almost a year since Laura died and yet just the sight of her name on an envelope was enough to remind him of her laughter and vitality. A year, and yet simply seeing his wife's name in print was all it took to prod the still raw wound inside him.

Angrily he crushed the catalogue between his fingers.

What right had companies to send out mail to people long since dead and buried? What right had they to remind relatives of the loved ones they had lost? Did they think he needed reminding? Did they think he'd ever forget?

And did his boss honestly believe he was the right person to wet-nurse a new member of staff? he wondered bitterly as his eyes fell on Hannah Blake's file again. The A and E department of St Stephen's Hospital in London was one of the busiest in the city, and certainly no place for any inexperienced girl.

Grimly he got to his feet and strode out of his office and down the corridor. Well, he'd give this new girl the facts of A and E life, but that was all he would do. The last thing he needed right now was a babysitting job.

Or Little Miss Muffet in a white coat, he groaned silently when he opened the staffroom door and saw the girl standing by the window.

'Dr Blake?' he asked, hoping he might be wrong.

'Yes, I'm Hannah Blake.' She nodded, turning eagerly towards him. 'And you are...?'

Old, he decided, as he stared at her elfin-shaped face and mop of curly golden-brown hair cut into a short bob. He'd just turned thirty-four the previous month, and yet suddenly he felt old, and tired, and jaundiced.

'I'm Robert Cunningham, special registrar,' he said quickly, seeing the eagerness in her face beginning to turn to uncertainty as her eyes took in his crumpled brown corduroys and shirt, and his dishevelled black hair.

Her smile returned and she held out her hand. 'I'm very pleased to meet you, sir.'

He ought to have told her that everyone called him Robert—he should have done—but all he could think as he continued to stare at her was that once, a very long time ago, he must have looked like this—optimistic, eager, keen. Once he must have believed the world was full of endless possibilities, and suddenly all he wanted to do was stamp on that youthful vitality, crush that idealism and enthusiasm, which seemed somehow to mock him.

'OK, there are four things to remember when you're working in A and E,' he declared, deliberately ignoring her outstretched hand. 'Anything you don't know, or aren't sure of, ask me or our SHO, Elliot Mathieson. Keep out from under my feet at all times, always erase the name of the last patient you've treated from the white board immediately, and everyone contributes fifty pence a week towards the cost of our coffee and biscuits, whether they take them or not.'

And with that he sat down, put his feet on one of the coffee-tables and pointedly closed his eyes.

'That's it?' she said faintly. 'I mean, I expected.... I rather hoped—'

'For a guided tour?' he said, opening one cold grey eye. 'A brass band—a welcome to St Stephen's buffet?'

A deep flush of colour stained her cheeks. 'No, of course not, but—'

'Dr Blake, according to your CV, you're a doctor. Unless that CV lied, I suggest you go away and do some doctoring and leave me to get some sleep in peace.'

And without waiting for her reply he closed his eyes again.

Well, her special registrar was a real charmer, and no mistake, Hannah decided as she walked out of the staffroom, only just resisting the impulse to slam the door behind her. Of course she hadn't expected a welcome mat but a little bit of civility wouldn't have cost him anything. A little bit of kindness wouldn't have killed him.

And she'd thought he'd looked quite nice, too, when he'd first opened the staffroom door. Not nice as in handsome—his features were far too sharp and angular for that—but nice as in approachable, understanding, and then he'd virtually told her to get lost.

A prickle of tears welled in her throat and she pulled a handkerchief from her pocket and angrily blew her nose. She hadn't cried since she was six years old and she wasn't about to start now because of one rude man with a shock of untidy black hair and a pair of cold grey eyes.

So what if Robert Cunningham clearly considered her the lowest form of medical life? And so what if the St Stephen's Infirmary looked even more dilapidated now than it had done when she'd come for her interview two months ago in June?

She'd wanted a junior post in London, in a hospital as far away from Edinburgh as she could get, and she'd got one. It was up to her to make a success of it, and everyone in this hospital couldn't be as rude as the special registrar.

They weren't.

The minute she stuck her head round the treatment-room door, a plump girl with thick black hair caught up into a high ponytail under her cap smiled a welcome. 'Can I help you at all, Doctor?'

'I hope so,' Hannah replied fervently. 'I'm Hannah Blake.'

The girl gazed at her blankly for a second, then clapped an apologetic hand to her forehead. 'Oh, cripes! Our consultant, Mr Mackay, did tell me you were starting on the 4th of August but I'm afraid I completely forgot. Jane Halden,' she continued, holding out her hand. 'Senior Sister in A and E for my sins. Flo, come and meet Dr Blake,' she called, beckoning to the tall, striking-looking black girl who had emerged from one of the cubicles. 'Dr Blake, this is Staff Nurse Floella Lazear, one of the best staff nurses in the business.'

'Flattery will get you nowhere, Jane!' The girl laughed. 'Nice to meet you, Doctor.'

'Please, call me, Hannah—both of you,' she insisted. 'Would either of you know where I might find Dr Mathieson? I really ought to introduce myself to him.'

'He's in cubicle 3 at the moment with Kelly Ross, our student nurse, examining a possible perforated appy,' Floella replied, 'but I wouldn't worry too much about introducing yourself to Elliot. Our SHO has a built-in homing device when it comes to new female members of staff.'

'A built-in homing device?' Hannah repeated, bewildered.

The staff nurse's deep brown eyes danced. 'Dr Mathieson may not be mad and bad, but he's most definitely dangerous to know, Hannah.'

'Oh, come on, Flo,' Jane protested. 'Elliot's great to work with...'

'And thirty-two-years old, blond, blue-eyed, and absolutely gorgeous,' the staff nurse grinned. 'Unfortunately he's also divorced with absolutely no intention of ever settling down again, so—'

'St Stephen's is littered with broken hearts,' Hannah finished for her with a laugh.

'Too right.' Floella nodded. 'If you're wanting fun with no commitment, Elliot's your man, but a long-term relationship? Forget it.'

If the staff nurse intended her comment as a warning, Hannah didn't need it. Being a useful member of the team was all she was interested in, and after what had happened with Chris... No, she didn't need any warning about handsome male doctors.

'You'll have met our consultant—Mr Mackay?' Jane queried.

Hannah nodded. 'I met him when I came for my interview. He seemed very nice.'

'He is,' the sister agreed. 'Though you probably won't see very much of him unless it's something really serious.

Robert Cunningham—our special reg—pretty much runs the show on a day-to-day basis, and—'

'I met him this morning,' Hannah interrupted. 'He seemed…he seemed a little tired when I saw him,' she said, determined to be charitable.

'Exhausted, more like.' Jane grimaced. 'God knows when that man last ate a decent meal, or had a good night's sleep. He practically lives in the department, and has done ever since…'

The rest of what Sister Halden had been going to say died on her lips as the doors to the treatment room suddenly banged open and two paramedics rushed in, pushing a trolley.

'Stabbing incident! BP 60 over 40, GCS 3-3-4. No breath sounds on the left side, so we tubed him, Doc!'

Doc.

He meant her, Hannah realised as Floella and Jane instantly slipped into their professional roles and began cutting off the young man's clothing and attaching him to a ventilator. He meant she should do something, and do it quickly. And why shouldn't he think that? She was the only one wearing a white coat, and she was the only one doing nothing.

'Do we know his name—age—anything?' she asked with a calmness she was very far from feeling.

'He's Ian Simpson, according to his wallet,' the paramedic replied. 'And at a guess I'd say he's between twenty-three and twenty-six.'

Quickly Hannah placed her stethoscope on the injured man's chest. The paramedic had been right. There were definitely no breath sounds on the left side. The young man's left lung had collapsed, and blood and air were seeping into his chest cavity.

'IV lines, Floella?' she asked.

The staff nurse glanced up at the drip bags containing

the saline solution which was temporarily providing a substitute for the blood Ian Simpson was losing. 'Open and running.'

'BP, Jane?'

'Still 60 over 40,' the sister replied as she connected the injured man to the cardiac monitor.

Sixty over forty was much too low, and Ian Simpson's GCS—his score of consciousness on the Glasgow coma scale—wasn't a whole lot better.

'Hannah?'

Jane Halden was gazing at her anxiously. The heart monitor was showing an increasingly uneven heart rhythm. With blood and air seeping into his chest cavity, Ian Simpson's heart was having to beat much too fast, trying to get enough oxygen to his brain, and if they didn't insert a chest drain—and fast—he could have a heart attack.

'Do you want me to page Robert?' the sister continued, clearly sensing Hannah's indecision.

And have him think she couldn't cope? Have him think—as he all too obviously already suspected—that she was useless? She'd watched a chest drain being inserted many times, had even performed a couple herself under supervision. Well, now was the time to find out whether she could do one alone.

'Chest tube and scalpel, please, Jane,' she said firmly.

The sister handed them to her and quickly Hannah made an incision into the upper right-hand side of Ian Simpson's chest, then carefully inserted a plastic tube directly into his chest cavity. With the tube hooked up to the suction line the excess air and blood was removed in seconds and the lung began to reinflate.

'Well done,' Jane murmured as Hannah let out the breath she hadn't even known she'd been holding. 'You'll be wanting six units of O-negative blood, a chest X-ray and a CBC?'

Hannah nodded. Type O blood could be given to any patient, buying them time until their blood samples had been tested. The X-ray would show whether she'd positioned the chest tube correctly, and the CBC—the complete blood count—would tell them just how much blood the patient had lost.

'OK, folks, what have we got here?'

Hannah spun round, startled, momentarily lost her balance and fell nose first against a broad, muscular chest. A broad, muscular chest which she was mortified to discover belonged to none other than Robert Cunningham.

'I'm so sorry, sir,' she began, whipping her hands quickly away from his chest. 'I didn't know you were there.'

'So it would appear,' he observed irritably. 'Perhaps I should wear a bell round my neck in future if you're as jumpy as this.'

Jumpy? She wasn't jumpy, but, then, neither had she expected to find herself noticing that, up close, the special registrar had eyes she was sure could smile if only he'd let them, and a mouth that looked just made for laughing if he'd only give it the chance.

'I'm sorry, what did you just say?' she asked, pulling her scattered wits together as she suddenly realised that Robert Cunningham had asked her something.

'I asked what was wrong with your patient,' he said tightly.

'It's a—a pneumothorax,' she stammered, wondering why on earth she should start wondering what the special registrar would look like if he smiled, 'but I've inserted a chest drain.'

His black eyebrows rose. 'You've done what?'

'You told me to go and do some doctoring so I have!' she retorted without thinking, only to flush deeply as his eyebrows rose. 'Dr Cunningham—'

'Have you remembered to order six units of O-negative, a chest X-ray and a CBC?'

Her chin came up at that. 'Of course.'

'Then, assuming you've inserted the chest drain correctly—'

Well, thanks a bundle for the vote of confidence, Hannah thought grimly.

'And assuming he doesn't have an unusual blood group, all you have to do now is to tell his family he's survived your ministrations. Where are they?'

'Th-they?' she faltered, her heart catapulting to the pit of her stomach as she realised the implication of his words.

'You did remember to ask the paramedics if anyone came in with him, didn't you?' he asked, his eyebrows snapping down.

The colour on her cheeks darkened to crimson. 'I... We... Everything was happening so fast, you see, and I...I...'

Her voice trailed away into mortified silence and Robert groaned inwardly. That was all he needed this morning. A new member of staff who not only looked as though she should be still at school but who was inefficient into the bargain.

'And how, may I ask, do you propose to discover if your unfortunate patient was accompanied by anyone?' he demanded, his voice ice-cold.

'The paramedics—'

'Will be long gone by now,' he snapped. 'Which means we'll either have to go out into the waiting room and ask everyone there if they came in with a stabbing incident, or perhaps you favour the more direct approach—an announcement over the Tannoy?'

Hannah's cheeks reddened even more. 'I'm sorry. I didn't think—'

'A fact that is all too blatantly obvious!' he retorted, and Jane Halden cleared her throat awkwardly.

'Robert, Hannah only arrived half an hour ago. Don't you think you're being a little harsh?'

Of course he was but, damn it, he didn't have time to babysit anyone. He'd never had to babysit Laura when she'd been his junior. She'd always known what to do. She'd—

'BP 60, neck veins swollen, no heart sounds!' Floella suddenly yelled.

Robert whirled back to the trolley. 'The pericardium—the sac round his heart—must be filling with fluids.'

'Will I page the chest surgeon?' Jane asked, reaching for the phone only to see Robert shake his head.

'This guy will be dead before the chest surgeon gets here.'

'Then what are we going to do?' Hannah asked, but Robert wasn't even listening to her. He'd already snapped on a pair of latex gloves, grabbed a scalpel from the trolley and, without a second's hesitation, made a wide incision across the young man's chest, slicing through the muscles to the ribs below.

He's going to do a thoracotomy, Hannah thought in amazement when he then took a large metal rib spreader, inserted it between two of Ian Simpson's ribs and spread them wide enough apart to get his hands into the chest cavity. It was a last-ditch effort, but if he pulled it off...

'BP now, Flo?' he demanded after he'd cut into the sac round Ian Simpson's heart and the trapped blood gushed out.

'Still falling!'

It shouldn't have been. Hannah could see the patient's heart beating more forcefully beneath Robert Cunningham's fingers so the blood pressure should have been going up, not down.

'There's a hole in his heart!' she exclaimed, suddenly seeing it. 'Lower right side. The knife must have pierced it when he was stabbed!'

Without a second's thought Robert inserted his finger into the hole and the flow of blood stopped instantly.

'BP now, Flo?' he asked.

'Eighty over sixty...ninety over seventy... You've got him, Robert!'

'Theatre ready?'

'On standby,' Jane replied.

'OK, Flo, let's go!'

And with Robert's finger still lodged in Ian Simpson's heart, Floella Lazear swiftly guided the trolley out of the cubicle and down the corridor, leaving Hannah gazing wistfully after them.

She would have liked to have gone, too. She would have been even happier if Robert Cunningham could have conceded she wasn't entirely useless, but he hadn't even glanced in her direction before he'd left.

'If you're hoping Robert will ever say "Well done", I'm afraid you'll wait until hell freezes over,' Jane murmured, clearly reading her mind. 'He's not being rude, it's just that he's always so focused on his work it never occurs to him to give praise.'

'He's good, isn't he?' Hannah sighed. 'At his job, I mean?'

Jane nodded. 'Brilliant. Unfortunately he can also be lethal if he thinks you're not pulling your weight, as poor Dr Jarvis discovered.'

'Dr Jarvis?' Hannah queried.

'Your predecessor. He only lasted two months with us before he handed in his resignation. He just couldn't cope, you see,' Jane added as Hannah stared at her in dismay. 'I don't think he realised how stressful working in A and E was going to be, and not everybody is up to it.'

Hannah fervently hoped she was. Robert Cunningham quite clearly was. She'd never seen anyone approach a thoracotomy as casually as he had done, for all the world as though he'd been doing nothing more exotic than removing someone's tonsils.

'Robert is one of the best in the business,' Jane continued, as though she'd read her mind. 'You'll learn a tremendous amount from him—we all have. I just wish...' She sighed and shook her head. 'I just wish he'd ease up a bit. He virtually lives at the hospital.'

'He's a workaholic, then?' Hannah suggested.

'He was always a very dedicated doctor, but ever since his wife was killed last year he virtually eats and sleeps A and E.'

'Had they been married long?'

Jane shook her head. 'Two years, that's all. Laura was a junior doctor in the department, and she was knocked down by a car right outside the hospital. Actually, it was pretty awful. Robert was on duty when they brought her in.'

'But that's dreadful,' Hannah gasped, truly shocked. 'He must have been devastated.'

'He was—is.' Jane nodded. 'And the trouble is, he won't let any of us help him. He won't talk about it or discuss it. All he does is work, and everybody knows that doesn't solve anything.'

Sometimes it did, Hannah thought pensively. Sometimes work could be a panacea for your troubles, as she knew only too well. 'Jane—'

'Hey, what's a nice girl like you doing in a place like this?'

Did every male doctor in this department walk like a cat? Hannah wondered as she turned to find herself gazing up into a pair of deep blue eyes. Deep blue eyes that were set in the handsome face of a man with blond hair. Elliot

Mathieson, she decided. It just had to be, and Jane Halden confirmed it.

'Elliot, that has to be the oldest chat-up line I've ever heard,' she protested, and he grinned.

'Fair's fair, Janey. I've been up to my elbows in a perforated appy for the last forty minutes. What did you expect—originality?'

'Something a whole lot better than that hairy old chestnut,' she said with a laugh. 'Hannah, this—if you haven't already guessed—is Elliot Mathieson, our SHO. Elliot, meet Hannah Blake, the latest recruit to the madhouse.'

'Pleased to meet you,' he declared, shaking her outstretched hand. 'Lord, but either I'm getting old, or you look terribly young.'

'I'm ageing by the minute, believe me,' she said with feeling, and he chuckled.

'Rough morning?'

'Not too bad,' she replied, but Elliot wasn't fooled for a second.

'Had a run-in with Robert already, have you?' he said shrewdly. 'Stand up to him, love. If you don't, he'll walk all over you.'

She squinted over her shoulder at her back. 'I think he already has.'

He laughed, then a slight frown appeared in his deep blue eyes. 'Hannah Blake. *Hannah* Blake? Look, I know this is going to sound really corny but could we possibly have met before?'

Oh, but she didn't need this, she thought, not on her first day. The department's consultant, Mr Mackay, knew who she was, and eventually—inevitably—everyone else would find out, too, but she'd hoped to have established herself, to have proved she was good at her job, before that happened.

She cleared her throat awkwardly but to her relief Jane unwittingly came to her rescue.

'You're right, Elliot. That was corny, and clichéd, and undoubtedly the *second* oldest chat-up line, I've ever heard!' she groaned.

The SHO stuck out his tongue at her. 'I'm trying my best, Janey.'

'In that case, maybe you should give up flirting,' she retorted, and Elliot winked at Hannah.

'She's secretly madly in love with me, you know.'

'Yeah, right, and I'm also six feet tall with a figure like a supermodel.' Jane laughed. 'Come on, Hannah. Elliot clearly needs time to think up some new chat-up lines, and you and I have work to do.'

Hannah chuckled as Jane bore her away, but her laughter died when she reached the end of the treatment room and glanced back to see that Elliot was staring after them, a decided frown on his forehead. How long would it be before the SHO remembered why her name sounded so familiar? A month—maybe less? And he would remember. She had no doubt about that.

But at least not today, she thought ruefully as the rest of her shift sped by in an exhausting and bewildering round of casualties. Nobody would have time even to think today, far less remember.

'Doesn't it ever ease up?' she protested when Floella stripped the cover off the examination trolley and replaced it with yet another one in preparation for the next patient. 'I've lost count of the number of casualties I've seen.'

'Wait until you do nights,' the staff nurse replied. 'Days are a picnic in comparison.'

Jane had told her earlier that weekends were a nightmare, and now Floella was saying that nights were murder too. Terrific, Hannah thought, trying and failing to ease the ache in her shoulders and back. She could hardly wait.

'Who's next?' she asked.

'A fifty-two-year-old homeless man, complaining of trouble with his leg. He's been living rough for the past ten years, so I'd better warn you—he's pretty ripe.'

Ripe wasn't the word Hannah would have used to describe the smell that emanated from the man Floella helped into the cubicle. Putrid was closer to the mark.

'I understand you're having bother with your leg, sir?' she said, trying unsuccessfully to hold her breath when the man clambered awkwardly up onto the trolley.

'I keeps falling over, ducks, and it ain't because I'm drunk.' He cackled, revealing a row of broken, discoloured teeth. 'Leastwise, not always.'

Hannah frowned as she took his blood pressure, pulse and temperature. His pupils were slightly dilated and his heart rate was unsteady. He might be only fifty-two, but he looked at least seventy, and unsteadiness on his feet could mean a stroke, or even heart problems.

The safest thing was to give him a complete examination. It would have been a task made considerably easier if he hadn't appeared to be wearing every stitch of clothing he possessed, but what really puzzled Hannah was why, with every layer she and Floella removed, a strange, unidentifiable aroma should become stronger.

'What *is* that smell?' she murmured out of the corner of her mouth as Floella gingerly placed yet another layer of filthy clothing on the cubicle floor.

The staff nurse shook her head. 'Beats me. Some new aftershave called City Streets, perhaps?'

It wasn't. When they finally removed the last of the homeless man's clothing the cause of the stench became all too horrifyingly clear. His leg was one huge, ugly, suppurating sore.

'Dear God!' Floella whispered, taking an involuntary

step back, and it took all Hannah's self-control not to run straight out of the cubicle.

'I...I'm afraid I'm going to have to send you up to one of our wards, sir,' she began. 'Your leg...' She took a deep breath and immediately wished she hadn't. 'It requires a lot more expert attention than I can give. I'll get a porter...'

'You mean I'm going to have to stay, ducks?' the man asked, his faded brown eyes lighting up. 'I'll have a bed for the night? So every cloud does have a silver lining!'

Hannah wondered where her particular silver lining had gone when she turned to summon a porter and saw Robert Cunningham watching her.

She hadn't seen him for at least a couple of hours, and something about the way he was leaning against the cubicle wall, his arms folded across his chest, told her she didn't want to see him now.

'Is there something wrong?' she asked as soon as one of the porters had wheeled the homeless man away.

'I won't insult your intelligence by asking if you've kept your tetanus and hepatitis shots up to date,' he observed, 'and you've at least remembered to put on latex gloves...'

'But?' she said stiffly.

'You didn't put a mask on that patient and he was coughing.'

She gazed at him in disbelief. 'Dr Cunningham, the man's leg was plainly gangrenous, and you're worried in case he might have a *cold*?'

He unfolded his arms and straightened up. 'I am, if it means he has TB.'

'TB?' she echoed faintly.

'Patients bring germs into A and E, Dr Blake. Hepatitis, HIV and TB, to name but three. We have a vaccine for hepatitis, and if you remember to wear gloves you should be safe from being accidentally infected with HIV, but TB is endemic amongst the homeless. Putting a mask on a patient who is coughing is the best—perhaps the only—way of preventing yourself from exposure.'

She opened her mouth, then closed it again. Even a third-year medical student would have remembered the dangers of TB. How could she have forgotten? How could she have been so stupid?

And Robert knew she had been stupid, and yet an unwelcome flicker of sympathy stirred inside him as he gazed down at her.

How old was she? Twenty-three—twenty four? She looked considerably younger with that ridiculous mop of hair, and it was clear from the redness of her cheeks that she didn't need another lambasting. What she really needed was someone to give her a hug, to tell her they'd all made mistakes at the start of their careers. Well, the hug was a definite no-no, but he could at least provide some encouragement.

'Look, Dr Blake—' he began gently, only to spin round as a piercing scream split the air. 'What the—?'

'The waiting room!' Hannah exclaimed. 'It sounded as though it came from the waiting room!'

It did, but as they ran through the waiting-room doors together Hannah came to a horrified halt when she saw the reason for the disturbance. Two drunks were fighting by the tea and coffee dispenser, while a third was casually urinating against the reception desk.

'Shocked, Dr Blake?' Robert murmured, hearing her sharp intake of breath.

Of course she was shocked, he thought as he gazed down at her white face. Only a man like him who had long since lost all feeling wouldn't have been, and Hannah was plainly sensitive. Sensitive and vulnerable with her big brown eyes and golden brown curls, and suddenly, inexplicably, he knew that he didn't want to see A and E destroying her freshness and enthusiasm. Didn't want to watch her becoming hardened and cynical as he knew she must to survive.

'This is child's play compared to what you'll have to face in the future, Dr Blake,' he continued as two security guards manhandled the drunks away and their receptionist began calming the waiting casualties. 'Fifteen—even ten years ago hospitals used to be regarded as sacred territory, but not any more. Now, doctors, nurses and porters are routinely threatened or attacked by gangs, disgruntled patients and psychotics.'

She glanced up at him. 'Are you trying to frighten me?'

His grey eyes held hers. 'Am I succeeding?'

She lifted her chin a notch. 'No.'

'Then you're a fool,' he said bluntly. 'The NHS doesn't award medals for bravery, and the staff who survive in A and E are the ones who possess a healthy sense of fear.'

Oh, she possessed a healthy sense of fear all right, Hannah thought ruefully, but it wasn't fear for her own safety. It was fear that in an emergency she might not be able to cope. In a crisis she might be found wanting.

And you're going to tell Robert Cunningham that, are you? a little voice asked at the back of her mind as she watched him walk back into the treatment room. You're going to tell him you're scared you'll fail?

Unconsciously she shook her head. No, she couldn't tell him that—she simply couldn't—but she also realised something else as she stared out over the still crowded waiting room.

It wasn't only the special registrar's good opinion that mattered. It was the people sitting there. The people who were in pain, the people who were unhappy, the people who were looking to her to help them.

Nobody had ever said this branch of medicine was easy. Nobody had promised it would be a bed of roses. She had chosen to specialise in A and E, and somehow—some way—she was going to have to cope. She had to. To be able to look Robert Cunningham in the eye, and maintain her own self-respect.

CHAPTER TWO

IT COULDN'T be anyone else, Hannah thought with dismay as she came to a halt in the middle of the pavement. The broad shoulders, the shock of unruly black hair, the way he was walking with his chin hunched deep into his shoulders. Robert Cunningham. Robert Cunningham walking so slowly that unless she made an immediate detour she'd catch up with him.

So, catch up with him, her mind urged. Since you came to St Stephen's a fortnight ago the man's scarcely said two words to you. Maybe he'd welcome the opportunity to talk. Maybe he only appears distant and aloof because he's still hurting over the death of his wife last year.

Yeah, right. And maybe this was really an incredibly bad idea, she decided when she quickened her pace and he greeted her cheery 'hello' with all the enthusiasm of someone stuck at a party with the world's biggest bore.

'I didn't know you lived around here,' he observed, managing to make his comment sound like an accusation and a condemnation at the same time.

'I've got one of the hospital flats in Leyland Court,' she replied, pointing to the drab grey building behind her. 'It looks a bit grim from the outside but the flats themselves aren't too bad.' Actually, they were dreadful. Minimum furniture, minimum comfort, maximum dreariness. Their sole advantage was their close proximity to St Stephen's. 'I understand you live in Wellington Place—in fact, we're practically neighbours—'

'Aren't you far too early for your shift?' he interrupted. 'Or has my watch stopped?'

'I always come in early. There aren't any private kitchens in the flats, you see,' she added as his eyebrows rose. 'And as the communal one gets a bit frantic in the morning I usually just pick up some coffee and toast in the canteen before I start work.'

'I see.'

'St Stephen's... It does the best breakfast in London.'

And why the heck was she bothering? she wondered when her voice trailed away into silence and he said nothing. He didn't want to hear about her eating habits. He obviously didn't want to hear anything she had to say, full stop. The best thing she could do was to make herself scarce, fast.

'I'd better go...'

'How are you settling in at the hospital?' he asked unexpectedly.

Was she supposed to think he cared? 'Fine, thank you.'

'No problems, then?' he pressed.

Lots. Like never seeming to get enough sleep. Like knowing she was surviving each day in A and E on a wing and a prayer. But the main problem at the moment, she thought ruefully, was Robert Cunningham obviously suddenly deciding he ought to talk to her. 'No problems, thank you, sir.'

'It's Robert,' he said irritably. 'Everyone calls me Robert.'

She knew that, but now didn't seem to be the time to point out he'd never actually told her to call him by his first name. 'I really ought to go—'

'Do they still serve fried bread in the canteen?' he interrupted.

'F-fried bread?' she stammered, then nodded.

'Then what are we waiting for?' he asked, surprising her for a second time. Hannah's surprise was as nothing to the total bewilderment Robert felt when he found himself standing in line at the hospital canteen.

What in the world was he doing here? he wondered, all too uncomfortably aware of the number of pairs of curious eyes fixed on him. Normally he just had strong black coffee for breakfast. Normally he avoided any kind of social contact with his colleagues like the plague.

It was all Hannah Blake's fault, he decided, glancing irritably across to where she'd found them an empty table by the window. If she hadn't looked so ill at ease talking to him. If he hadn't found himself suddenly feeling guilty for the way he'd been ignoring her since she'd come to St Stephen's...

And was it any wonder he felt guilty? Little Miss Muffet who looked as though a puff of wind would blow her away. Little Miss Muffet with her snub nose, too-large brown eyes and skin so pale he suspected a kiss would bruise it.

Not that he ever had any intention of finding out. Good God, no. He wasn't looking for a relationship, and, even if he had been, cradle-snatching had never been in his line. He simply felt sorry for her, he told himself firmly, as he would have for any junior doctor new to A and E. And someone had to make sure she was starting an eight-hour shift with something more substantial than a cup of coffee and some toast in her stomach.

'That isn't what I ordered,' she protested when he arrived at the table carrying two heavily laden plates of the St Stephen's special.

'You need feeding up.'

'But—'

'Eat,' Robert ordered, putting one of the plates down in front of her.

'Aye aye, sir,' she muttered, but he heard her.

'Insubordination, Dr Blake?'

That was very nearly a joke, she thought in amazement,

and sure enough, when she glanced up at him, there was actually a ghost of a smile playing round his lips.

'Mutiny, more like,' she observed wryly. 'If I eat even half of that I'll be comatose by eleven.'

'Not with our workload, you won't. Look, Dr Blake—'

'My name's Hannah,' she interrupted, 'and if you're worried in case I'm either too poor to buy myself breakfast or anorexic, you can relax. I've never eaten much for breakfast and I've always been thin.'

Skinny would have been a much more accurate description, he thought critically. Skinny, and pale, and he'd bet money those dark shadows under her eyes weren't smudges of mascara.

'Hannah, nobody can work a sixty-hour week and study at the same time if they're not eating properly,' he insisted, then bit his lip. He was beginning to sound like her mother. He'd be asking her next if she was getting enough sleep, remembering to wrap up warm. 'And we're short-staffed enough in A and E as it is, without you suddenly going off sick,' he added brusquely.

The smile that had been lurking in her eyes died. 'I'm sorry,' she murmured, picking up her knife and fork. 'I'll try my best not to inconvenience you by becoming ill.'

Which was all he was interested in, he told himself, so why did he suddenly feel like a complete and utter heel? And he did as he watched her silently beginning to eat her breakfast. She hadn't asked him to join her—he'd invited himself—and what had he done? Supplied her with a breakfast she didn't want, and made her feel guilty into the bargain.

'Look, are you really settling in all right in A and E?' he asked before he had time to consider the wisdom of his question.

'Of course I am,' Hannah began brightly, then sighed a little wryly when his eyebrows rose. 'OK—all right—I'll admit it's a lot more immediate than I'd expected. One minute you're dealing with a splinter in somebody's finger, the next it's a possible heart attack.'

'And with no medical records to go on, "What's wrong with the patient?" can all too quickly become "What did the patient die of?"' He nodded. 'The trick is to become very skilled at asking the right kind of questions.'

'Yes, but even asking someone "How badly does it hurt?" doesn't help a lot when pain is such a very personal thing,' she exclaimed, forking some egg into her mouth. 'I mean, what you might find quite bearable, I could say was excruciating.'

Robert doubted it. She might look as though a puff of wind would blow her away but now that he was looking at her—*really* looking—he could see a hint of stubbornness about her jaw despite her apparent fragility, a determination in her large brown eyes he hadn't noticed before. Miss Muffet had backbone. The big question was whether she had enough.

'I think the best advice I can give is always think the worst,' he observed, taking a sip of his coffee. 'Rule that out first, then you can safely move on to investigate other possibilities.'

It was good advice. What amazed her most was that it was Robert Cunningham who was giving it. Robert Cunningham, whose habitual response to any question she'd asked since she'd arrived at St Stephen's had been a brusque, 'Ask Elliot.'

He looked different, too, today, she decided, though she couldn't for a moment figure out why. His faded green shirt was just as crumpled as all the other shirts he normally wore, and though his corduroys were black this morning instead of brown, that hardly explained the difference.

It was because he was smiling, she suddenly realised. OK, so it wasn't a full-blown, right-up-to-the eyes effort, but it was still a smile and she'd been right when she'd thought it would change him. It made him look considerably younger and quite unexpectedly attractive. His hair badly needed cutting, of course, and his shirt could have done with an iron...

And you need your eyes tested if you think this man's attractive, her mind protested. Elliot Mathieson's an attractive man. Robert Cunningham's a mess. Yes, but a mess with a very nice smile when he chooses to use it.

'And don't ever be afraid to ask for help,' Robert continued, clearly taking her silence to mean just that. 'Nobody expects you to be an expert when you're first starting out.'

Kindness, understanding from Robert Cunningham? Wonders would never cease, she thought in amazement. In fact, if he was going to be this accommodating perhaps she might actually be able to start relaxing at St Stephen's.

And then again, perhaps not, she thought, her heart skipping a beat when he suddenly added, 'According to your CV, you were born in Edinburgh, and did all your training there. What brought you to London? I mean, wouldn't it have made more sense to look for your first post in your home town?'

'I wanted a change of scene,' she replied lightly, 'and as I used to come to London a lot for holidays when I was a little girl, I thought, why not?'

It had been the answer she and Mr Mackay, the consultant in charge of A and E, had agreed upon, and none of the rest of the staff had ever queried it, but, then, none of them, as she quickly discovered, was Robert Cunningham.

'You have relatives here, then?' he pressed. 'If you came often when you were a child...?'

'Not relatives, no,' she floundered. 'My father...he just happened to like London.'

A slight frown appeared in his dark grey eyes. 'It still seems rather a long way to come on the strength of holiday memories. Personally, I'd have thought starting a new job was enough of an upheaval without uprooting yourself as well.'

'Like I said, I wanted a change,' Hannah declared, striving to sound casual, dismissive, only to feel her cheeks heating up under his steady gaze. Why, oh, why did she always have to blush at the most inconvenient moments? It was a childish habit she should have outgrown years ago. 'And it seemed the right moment to make the break.'

'Yes, but—'

'Good grief, is that the time?' she interrupted, getting to her feet. 'We'd better go, or we'll be late for the start of our shift.'

She was right, they would, but Robert's frown deepened as he followed her out of the canteen and into A and E. Hannah Blake wasn't telling the truth about why she'd come to St Stephen's. She had a secret—a secret she didn't want discovered—and he didn't like secrets, never had. Secrets meant guilt. Secrets meant complications, and A and E had no room for either.

'Hannah, about this decision of yours to come to London—'

'RTA on the way, Robert!' Jane called. 'ETA five minutes.'

'Injuries?' he demanded, instantly focused.

'One female aged twenty-nine with minor cuts and bruises,' the sister replied, 'and a six-year-old girl with chest and head injuries. I've alerted the chest surgeon in case we need him, told Theatre to be on standby, and Jerry's on his way down from radiology.'

Robert started towards the treatment room door, then glanced back at Hannah. 'Would you like to assist me on this one?'

She gazed at him, open-mouthed. Did he mean it or

was he joking? The question was academic. Robert Cunningham didn't joke. 'You bet!' she breathed.

'Just remember—'

'To keep out from under your feet at all times.' She nodded. 'I haven't forgotten.'

A faint smile appeared in his eyes. 'Actually, I was going to say, if we need to intubate the little girl would you like to tackle it?'

'Oh— Right— Of course,' she replied, mentally kicking herself. 'I thought…when you said—'

'Hannah, will you relax?' he said gently. 'I'm not an ogre, you know.'

Perhaps not, she thought with a sigh as the ambulance arrived, its siren wailing, but he certainly could give a pretty good impression of being one at times.

'The kid and her mother are in London for a few days' holiday,' one of the paramedics announced as he and his colleague transferred the little girl from the stretcher onto the trolley. 'They were coming down The Mall when some maniac sideswiped their car, then took off.'

'Wonderful,' Robert commented dryly as Floella began inserting more IV lines to carry the O-negative blood which had already arrived, and Jerry Clark wheeled in his portable X-ray machine. 'Jerry, I'd like X-rays of her chest, pelvis and cervical spine. Hannah—'

'Get ready to intubate.' She nodded.

The little girl's head might be covered in blood, and her kneecap protruding at a grotesque angle through her skin, but the first priority was to regulate her breathing. At the moment it was ragged and uneven, and if they didn't alleviate it her brain would start to swell because of the reduced oxygen it was receiving.

'Are you ready, Hannah?' Robert asked, after he'd inserted a catheter into the child's urethra to drain her bladder

and given her an injection to temporarily sedate and para-
lyse her.

She nodded. Once Robert opened the front of the cervical
collar round the little girl's neck, and pressed down firmly
on the cricoid cartilage so her stomach contents couldn't
reflux into her airway, they'd have to work fast.

'I'm ready,' she said.

'OK, let's go,' he ordered.

Swiftly Hannah inserted the laryngoscope blade into the
girl's mouth and suctioned away the blood and saliva ob-
scuring her vocal cords. Then very gently she eased the
endotracheal tube past her vocal cords and down into the
child's trachea.

'Everything OK, Hannah?' Robert murmured.

It felt all right, it seemed all right, and she placed her
stethoscope on the child's chest and listened. Bingo! She
was breathing deeply and evenly without effort.

'Everything's fine,' she replied with relief.

'Is the haematocrit back on those blood samples yet?'
Robert demanded. Floella held out the results to him, but
to Hannah's surprise he waved them towards her. 'What
have we got, Hannah?'

Quickly she scanned the results. 'Red cell count very
low. How's her BP?'

'Stable,' Floella called.

'X-rays of the chest, pelvis and cervical spine are ready,
too, Robert,' Jerry declared, but again, to Hannah's bewilderment, the special registrar nodded towards her.

'Any problems, Hannah?' he asked, snaking an orogas-
tric tube into the little girl's mouth, past the endotracheal
tube and into her oesophagus to empty her stomach.

'Two broken ribs—pelvis fine, cervical spine fine. On
the evidence of these I'd say she should probably have a
CT scan to check out those head injuries before she goes
to Theatre, but…'

'But?' Robert prompted, his eyes fixed on her.

'To be perfectly honest, I'm not sure,' she admitted. 'It's her stomach, you see. It looks very firm to me, and it also seems slightly distended.'

'So?' Robert pressed.

Hannah took a deep breath. If she was wrong, so be it. If she looked like an idiot, she'd survive.

'I think the haematocrit result is too low for the amount of blood the child seems to have lost. I think she could be bleeding into her stomach and I'd send her to Theatre right away.'

For a moment Robert said nothing, then he smiled—a real, honest-to-goodness smile. 'So would I. Well done.'

He'd praised her, she thought in amazement as Floella and one of the porters wheeled the little girl out of the cubicle. She couldn't believe it, but he'd actually praised her.

'If your smile was any bigger I'd say you'd just won the lottery,' Jane observed, meeting her as she made her way to the white board to erase the child's name. 'Care to explain why?'

Hannah's smile widened as Robert strode past them and into cubicle 3 to talk to the child's mother. 'Would you believe hell just froze over?'

'Hell just...?' Jane gazed at her in confusion, then shook her head. 'Insanity. Normally it takes two to three months for people working in A and E to succumb—'

'Succumb to what?' Elliot asked curiously, overhearing her.

'Insanity,' Jane declared. 'Poor Hannah here. Right as rain two weeks ago and now...' She sighed and shook her head mournfully. 'Completely nuts, like the rest of us.'

Quickly Elliot clasped Hannah's wrist between his fingers and consulted his watch. 'Pulse rate fast and erratic, silly smile on her face... Yup, it looks like insanity to me, but I'd have to make a full examination to be sure. How about my place, tonight, eight o'clock?'

'Elliot, I said the girl was nuts, not stupid!' Jane exclaimed and Hannah chuckled as the sister hurried to answer the phone.

'I think I'll give the examination a miss, Elliot.' Hannah smiled.

'Do I look like the sort of man who'd take advantage?' he protested, his blue eyes wide and innocent.

'Elliot, you look like the man who wrote the book on how to!' She laughed.

'Too true,' he teased with a wickedly handsome grin. 'So your mother warned you about men like me, did she?'

Her smile became a little crooked. 'My mother died when I was born so she didn't have time to warn me about anything.'

His own laughter died instantly. 'Hannah, I'm sorry...I didn't know—'

'It's OK,' she interrupted. 'I never knew her, and people keep telling me you don't miss what you've never had.'

'And people who make observations like that deserve to be hung, drawn and quartered,' he declared, putting his arms around her and giving her a hug. 'Extremely slowly.'

She chuckled but she didn't move out of his arms. He was hugging her with sympathy and understanding, and she accepted the gesture in the spirit it was given.

Robert clearly didn't. In fact, judging from his thunderous expression when he emerged from cubicle 3 and saw them, he didn't appreciate the gesture at all.

'I think we'd better get back to work,' she murmured, quickly extricating herself from Elliot's arms. 'The boss doesn't look too happy about us wasting time.'

Elliot glanced over his shoulder at Robert and an amused smile curved his lips. 'Oh, I don't think that's what's bugging him, sweetheart.'

'You don't?' she said, puzzled, and he shook his head.

'It's jealousy, love,' he whispered. 'Pure, unadulterated, green-eyed jealousy.'

A splutter of laughter came from her as Elliot strolled away. Robert Cunningham *jealous*? If Elliot believed that then insanity wasn't simply common in A and E, it was endemic, but, judging by Robert's grim expression as he began walking towards her, now wasn't the time to discuss it. Now was the time for a very swift retreat, and Paul Weston in cubicle 6, with acute back pain according to the white board, fitted the bill perfectly.

'I feel so stupid, Doctor,' the young man declared the moment he saw her. 'I was helping my sister move some furniture yesterday, and now I can hardly move.'

'Which part of your back actually hurts?' Hannah asked, pulling up a chair to sit level with him.

'Down near the bottom—sort of to the left. And I'm feeling a bit sick, too.'

Warning bells went off in her head immediately. Nausea coupled with back pain could mean pyelonephritis—an inflammation of the kidneys—or even chronic kidney failure.

Robert had said she should always think the worst, she remembered, and she fully intended to.

'Have you been passing less urine recently, Mr Weston?' she asked, quickly taking his pulse.

'Yes, but—'

'Felt feverish at all—lethargic—as though you were coming down with flu?'

'Doctor, I only came in because I pulled a muscle in my back,' he protested.

Maybe he had. His pulse rate wasn't high, and his temperature and blood pressure were near normal, too, and yet...

'I'd like to do a few tests, Mr Weston,' she declared, getting quickly to her feet. 'Just as a precaution.'

'If you say so,' he murmured reluctantly, 'but could you give me something for this pain while I wait? I'm in absolute agony.'

A painkilling injection wouldn't affect the results of any tests she performed so swiftly she administered one, then went to phone the lab. Speed was of the essence if Paul Weston was suffering from chronic kidney failure, and she wanted to ensure there'd be no delay over any samples she took.

'Something wrong?' Jane asked, seeing Hannah frown as she put down the phone.

'Could be. Look, are you free right now, Jane? I need to take some blood and urine samples.'

'No problem.' The sister nodded. 'Where's your patient?'

'Cubicle 6.'

Jane stopped in mid-stride. 'Cubicle 6's empty. The guy who was in there left a couple of minutes ago.'

'But he can't have left,' Hannah protested, bewildered. 'He could hardly walk!'

'Believe me, that guy could have qualified for the next Olympic games, judging by the speed he left the treatment room,' the sister declared. 'What were you treating him for?'

'Back pain.'

Jane rolled her eyes heavenwards and groaned. 'And you gave him some painkiller. Oh, Hannah, drug addicts always insist they're suffering from either back pain or migraine because they know damn well there isn't a lab test or X-ray in the world which can disprove it. It's one of the oldest tricks in the book.'

Known to everybody but me, Hannah thought wretchedly. It had never occurred to her—not even for a second.

'Look, forget it,' Jane continued, seeing her expression.

'We've all been conned at least once in our professional careers.'

Not Robert Cunningham, Hannah thought as she suddenly saw him and realised he must have heard every word. Robert Cunningham had probably never been conned even when he'd been a student doctor.

He would think her so stupid and naïve. She felt both as she miserably erased Paul Weston's name from the white board. And Paul Weston probably hadn't even been his real name. That would be as fictitious as the symptoms he'd given her.

'Hannah—'

'You don't have to say anything, Robert,' she said, turning to him quickly. 'I know I've been a fool—'

'The first drug addict I ever treated told me he had kidney stones,' he interrupted. 'He had every symptom right down to blood in his urine. I sent a sample off to the lab, but the poor bloke was in such pain I gave him morphine while he waited. When the lab report came back there was blood in his sample all right. Chicken blood.'

'*Chicken* blood!' she gasped. 'But your patient—'

'Disappeared, having got what he came for. It's happened to all of us, Hannah, so don't lose any sleep over it.' He turned to go, then a slight smile curved his lips. 'Oh, by the way, I've just had word back from Theatre. You were right about that little girl who came in. She *was* bleeding into her stomach, but she should be all right, thanks to you.'

Why on earth had she ever thought him aloof and arrogant? she wondered as he walked away. He was kind and nice, and when he smiled like that, and his dark grey eyes didn't have those lurking shadows in them, he could be very nice indeed.

It was the single bright moment in a day that turned into

an unremitting round of chest pains, broken limbs, and accidental poisonings.

'Thank God we've only got another half-hour to go,' she told Floella as she binned yet another pair of latex gloves. 'I'm absolutely shattered.'

'Snap,' the staff nurse said laughing. 'And I'm afraid it looks like we've got another big one. Thirty-six-year-old male, very bad gash on his right hand, according to Reception.'

To Hannah's relief, however, the wound looked considerably worse than it actually was.

'It only needs a few stitches,' she told the plump, florid-faced, middle-aged man after she'd examined him. 'I'll get Staff Nurse Lazear to clean it for you, then I'll insert some sutures.'

'No.'

'You won't feel a thing, honestly,' she said reassuringly. 'I'll give you something to deaden the pain—'

'I'm not bothered about the pain,' he interrupted with irritation. 'I just don't want that black touching me.'

Hannah paused in the middle of filling her syringe and turned slowly to face him. 'I beg your pardon?'

'That black. I don't want her touching me. I want somebody else.'

'Well, it may surprise you to learn that this is not a supermarket where you can pick and choose,' Hannah said tightly. 'Staff Nurse Lazear is one of our most experienced nurses—'

'I don't care how experienced she is,' the man snapped. 'I want somebody else.'

'And perhaps you'd prefer to bleed to death!' Hannah flared.

The man levered his not inconsiderable bulk upright and Floella tugged quickly at Hannah's sleeve. 'Look, I really don't mind asking Jane to help you—'

'You'll do no such thing!' Hannah exclaimed. 'He'll have his hand cleaned by you, or he can leave right now!'

'You can't do that,' the man protested. 'You doctors have taken a…a hypocrite's oath to help people.'

'Our Hippocratic oath requires we help members of the human race, sir,' Hannah threw back at him. 'And right now I don't think you come even close to qualifying!'

The man's florid face reddened alarmingly. 'Why, you stuck-up little bitch! I'll teach you—'

'OK, what's going on in here?' Robert demanded, throwing open the cubicle curtains, his eyes cold, his face taut.

'This…this gentleman—and, believe me, I'm using the word extremely loosely,' Hannah replied icily, 'seems to have a problem with our nursing staff.'

'I don't have any problem,' the man exclaimed. 'I just don't want any black treating me.'

Robert stared at him silently for a second, then stepped out into the treatment room and beckoned to Elliot. 'Could you take over in here for Dr Blake, please, Dr Mathieson?'

'Now, just a minute,' Hannah protested as the SHO nodded. 'This is my patient—'

'Not any more, he's not,' Robert declared, gripping her so firmly by the elbow that, short of kicking his shins, there was nothing she could do but accompany him out of the cubicle and down the treatment room.

Which didn't mean she had to like it, and when he released her she turned on him angrily. 'You had no right to do that!'

'I'm the special registrar—I can do whatever I like,' he said calmly. 'Now, why don't we go to the staffroom, have a nice cup of tea—'

'I don't want a cup of tea!' she stormed. 'I want to know why you pulled me out of there. Why you let that jerk get away with what he said!'

'I did not let him get away with it.'

'You sent in Elliot—'

'And did I ask Flo to leave?' he demanded. 'Did I?'

'No, but—'

'Hannah, that man was going to hit you, and the only way to defuse the situation was to send in somebody with a much cooler head.'

She bit her lip. Robert was right. She'd lost her temper, and she shouldn't have.

'OK, I admit I handled the situation badly,' she muttered, 'but I don't need protecting. I can take care of myself.'

Dear God, he thought, if she believed that, then it wasn't a babysitter she needed but a bodyguard. 'Hannah, London isn't Edinburgh—'

'And Edinburgh isn't some quaint Highland village where we all leave our front doors open and never lock our cars,' she exploded. 'We have Aids, a huge drugs problem—'

'Which didn't help you when you met a real drug addict, did it?'' he retorted, then sighed when she coloured. 'Look, as you clearly have a very volatile temper, I think it might be better if I restrict you to treating female patients for a while until you learn how to control it.'

Her jaw dropped. 'You can't be serious!'

'My decision, Hannah,' he declared. 'And it's non-negotiable,' he added in a tone that brooked no opposition.

She opened her mouth, then clenched her teeth together until they hurt. She'd been right the first time. He wasn't nice. He was arrogant, and obnoxious, and stupid, but much as she longed to say so she knew she couldn't.

'Very well, *sir*,' she said instead. 'May I go now?'

'Hannah—'

'I've still got five minutes of my shift left, and with any luck I might be able to find some frail little old lady or a five-year-old child, you think I can safely treat!'

'Hannah, wait—'

But she didn't wait. She simply strode past him, her cheeks red, her back ramrod stiff with anger, leaving him gazing impotently after her.

'Everything OK now, boss?' Elliot asked as he emerged from cubicle 2, and Floella escorted Hannah's clearly very chastened patient back to the waiting room.

'*OK*?' Robert repeated. 'Elliot, that damn girl is going to get herself killed!'

'Yeah, she's feisty enough.' The SHO grinned.

'*Feisty*? Of all the knuckle-headed, irresponsible—'

'And you're always Mr Calm, are you?' Elliot observed, but Robert didn't smile back.

'She says she can take care of herself,' he fumed, as though the SHO hadn't spoken. 'She says she doesn't need protecting!'

Elliot's blue eyes became suddenly thoughtful. 'Ah.'

'Standing up to a bully like that—good God, Elliot, he must have outweighed her by at least fifty kilos!'

'Stupid.' Elliot nodded. 'Definitely stupid.'

Robert thrust his fingers through his black hair in exasperation. 'What am I going to do with her, Elliot? When I think of what could have happened, what undoubtedly *will* happen…'

The SHO's mouth turned up at the corners. 'Yeah, she is kinda cute, isn't she?'

'*Cute*?' Robert spluttered. '*Cute*?'

Desperately he tried to think of something swingeing, sarcastic, to retort but failed miserably—and to his acute irritation was reduced to walking away in disgust, much to Elliot's obvious amusement.

'What's so funny, Elliot?' Jane asked as she came out of the office and saw him laughing.

'Nothing yet, Janey. But in a couple of months' time, maybe less…' His blue eyes sparkled. 'I think life around here could get really interesting!'

CHAPTER THREE

'I HATE afternoon shifts,' Floella grumbled. 'Starting at three, finishing at eleven. By the time I get home my husband and kids are in bed, and I'm too exhausted to do anything.'

'I hate nights,' Hannah observed, following her and Jane across the street towards the entrance to St Stephen's. 'Trying to sleep during the day, all the drunks to look forward to at night—'

'Yes, but afternoon's—'

'Hey, will you two lighten up?' Jane protested. 'It's a beautiful September afternoon. There's not a cloud in the sky…'

'And not a window in A and E for us to admire it from,' Floella pointed out. 'I want to win the lottery and never have to work again. I want to travel the world and meet people who wouldn't recognise a stomach pump if they fell over one, far less know how to use it.'

And I want Robert Cunningham to get off my back, Hannah thought irritably as they walked through the treatment-room doors and she saw him deep in conversation with Elliot.

Ever since the SHO had quite rightly pointed out that the department couldn't function properly if they restricted her to treating female patients, Robert had been like a bear with a sore head. Nit-picking, carping, hovering about her if she got anywhere near a male casualty, and it was driving her slowly and completely mad.

So talk to him, her mind urged. Tell him you're not an

idiot, that you know what you're doing, and you won't take unnecessary risks.

Yeah, right, she thought ruefully as she hung up her jacket and turned to see Robert watching her, a deep frown pleating his forehead. Frankly, cutting your own throat would be an easier and far less painful way of solving your current problems.

'You know, once—just once—I'd like to come to work and find the waiting room completely empty,' Floella grumbled, glancing through the stack of notes which had come through from Reception.

'Not a hope, I'm afraid,' Jane sighed. 'Any priority?'

'The fourteen-year-old in cubicle 3, I'd say,' the staff nurse observed. 'Complaining of shortness of breath. History of asthma, according to his mother, and none of his usual medications seem to be working.'

They weren't. The teenager was gasping and gulping for air, and his fingers and lips were blue, a clear sign of cyanosis.

'How long has he been like this?' Hannah asked the boy's mother after she'd sounded his chest.

'About an hour,' the woman replied, panic plain in her eyes. 'I phoned our doctor and when I told him how drowsy he was, not seeming to know where he was—'

'Pulse 130 over 65,' Floella murmured.

Hannah turned to the teenager's mother with what she hoped was an encouraging smile. 'Wouldn't you be a lot more comfortable in one of our private waiting rooms? There's tea, coffee—'

'I want to stay with my son.'

'I know you do,' Hannah said soothingly, beckoning to their student nurse, Kelly Ross. 'But there's really nothing you can do here, and I promise we'll let you know what the situation is as soon as we can.'

The boy's mother reluctantly allowed the student nurse to lead her away.

The drowsiness and disorientation she'd noticed in her son, coupled with his rapid pulse rate, meant that too much carbon dioxide was building up in the boy's blood. They needed to take a pulse ox. to determine how much oxygen was left in his blood, and though the procedure wasn't a frightening one—it simply involved slipping a small plastic clip onto his finger containing an electrode which could read the oxygen content directly through his skin—the results would determine just how ill he was.

And with a pulse ox. of 82 he was very ill indeed.

Swiftly Hannah reached for an endotracheal tube to ease the teenager's laboured breathing. Once—oh, it seemed like a lifetime ago now—she would have approached this particular procedure with trepidation, but not any more. Now it was all too unfortunately commonplace.

'You'll be wanting a chest X-ray, CBC and a coag. panel?' Floella said, once the tube was in place and she'd set up an IV line and attached cardiac electrodes to the boy's chest to monitor his heartbeat.

Hannah nodded. The chest X-ray would reveal if there was any damage to the boy's lungs. The CBC would tell them how many red and white blood cells there were in his blood, and the coag. panel would test his body's ability to clot.

'Everything OK in here?'

Hannah gazed heavenwards with disbelief. Good grief, didn't Robert Cunningham trust her to treat even teenage boys now?

'Everything's fine, thank you,' she replied curtly.

'BP 160 over 95, pulse 140,' Floella announced.

Well, perhaps not exactly fine, Hannah amended mentally. The teenager's heart was working much too fast, trying to compensate for the low level of oxygen in his blood, and they had to stabilise him quickly.

'OK, Flo, I want epi. and solumedrol intravenously, and albuterol through the ET tube,' she declared.

The staff nurse nodded. With luck the epinephrine—the adrenaline—would regulate the boy's blood pressure and pulse, while the solumedrol and albuterol should ease his breathing.

'I presume you've taken samples for a CBC and a coag. panel?' Robert observed.

'You presume correctly,' Hannah replied, trying—and failing—to keep the edge out of her voice as Jerry Clark appeared with his X-ray equipment. 'Chest X-rays only, please, Jerry.'

'Anything for you, Hannah, love,' he replied, then added with a knowing leer, 'and I do mean *anything*.'

Of course he did, the little creep, but she managed to smile back. Slapping the smirk off his face would have been infinitely more preferable, but she'd very quickly learned that if you were a junior female doctor at St Stephen's, and wanted your X-rays processed fast, you had to put up with Jerry's clumsy attempts at flirtation.

Robert obviously didn't agree with her. In fact, judging by his icy expression, Jerry was lucky not to be sailing out of the cubicle by the seat of his pants.

Which would have suited Hannah just fine until she noticed Robert was throwing her a glance of equally arctic proportions. Did he think she actually *liked* toadying to an odious little creep like Jerry? She wouldn't have touched the X-ray technician with a bargepole, but as she was neither a male doctor nor a special registrar she couldn't afford to be antagonistic.

'His BP and pulse are coming down,' Floella murmured. 'I think he's stabilising, Hannah.'

The teenager was. His fingers and lips weren't nearly so blue, and his breathing was a lot less laboured.

'Are the coag. panel and CBC results back yet, Flo?' she asked.

The staff nurse handed them over to her. There was nothing in them to suggest anything other than a very severe asthma attack, neither did the teenager's X-rays show any sign of lung damage, but the quicker he was in Intensive Care the happier Hannah would be.

'That must be our fourth asthma case in the last three days,' Jane commented as Floella and one of the porters wheeled the teenager out of the treatment room on his way to IC.

Hannah nodded. 'I was reading an article the other day that said asthma was on the increase because so many of our houses are centrally heated. That, coupled with wall-to-wall carpeting—'

'And when the two of you have quite finished discussing interior design you might remember that we have a full waiting room of patients out there!'

Hannah's jaw dropped as Robert strode past them, his face tight and angry. She and Jane had taken a five-second breather. Five miserable, measly seconds to discuss what might cause asthma. There had been no need for him to be so rude, no need at all.

'I'd keep out of Robert's way for the rest of the afternoon, if I were you,' Jane murmured, clearly reading her thoughts. 'And if you need any help, ask Elliot.'

'Too damn right I will,' Hannah said tartly. 'Honestly, Jane, that man—'

'Hannah, his wife was knocked down and killed exactly a year ago tonight.'

'Oh, God, no,' Hannah gasped, turning quickly in time to see Robert disappearing into cubicle 8. 'No wonder he's being so difficult. Is there nothing we can do—nothing we can say—that would help?'

'Just keep out of his way,' Jane declared. 'Believe me, he won't thank you for anything else.'

Perhaps not, Hannah thought as their shift sped by. She followed Jane's suggestion, consulting Elliot if she needed any advice, closing her ears to the sound of Robert's snapped, caustic orders, but her heart went out to him every time she saw him.

How must he feel today? How would she feel if it were her? Desolate, shattered, bitter. There had to be something she could say that would help ease his grief, but any conversation she attempted was met by such a vehement rebuff that when a Miss Sheila Vernon came in shortly after ten o'clock with severe stomach pains, Hannah's heart sank into her boots.

'I don't suppose you could manage on your own, could you?' Floella grimaced when she asked her to go and get Robert. 'I know Elliot's all tied up with that OD, but Robert's on such a short fuse tonight, and asking for help...'

There was no alternative, Hannah thought grimly. She couldn't see inside Sheila Vernon's stomach to confirm or rule out anything, so palpation was the first line of investigation, and she knew she didn't possess the necessary skill to do it. She'd have to ask Robert for help, and if he chose to make her look ridiculous for requesting it, she'd just have to grit her teeth and bear it.

To her amazement, however, Robert neither took the opportunity to slip in a sarcastic comment about her lack of ability nor subjected her to withering scorn. In fact—if she hadn't known better—she could almost have sworn he was pleased to help her when she admitted her problem.

'The secret of successful palpation is never to rush,' he explained. 'The slower you press into the stomach, the more chance you'll have of seeing the patient "guarding"—trying to push your hand away when you press on a particularly sensitive area—which can help pinpoint the source of the pain.'

Hannah nodded.

'People who come into A and E with severe stomach pain always think they have appendicitis,' he observed as he began pressing gently across Sheila Vernon's stomach, 'but it's actually quite rare—less than four per cent of all cases—and Miss Vernon quite clearly doesn't have it or we'd be scraping her off the ceiling by now.'

Floella smothered a chuckle but Hannah, he noticed, didn't even smile.

He wasn't surprised. After his earlier jibe at her for wasting time she was hardly likely to be feeling very charitable towards him, but how she could tolerate the slimy overtures of a man like Jerry Clark was beyond him.

Laura wouldn't have tolerated it for a second. Laura would have drawn herself up to her full five feet nine and given Jerry one flash of her violet blue eyes, and if that hadn't intimidated the scumbag, she'd have hit him.

'Pulse and BP both dropping, Robert,' Floella warned.

'OK, get me a urine analysis, a guiac test on her stools and a liver function test, a.s.a.p.,' he ordered.

So why on earth had Hannah put up with it? he wondered as he began palpating the lower left quadrant of Sheila Vernon's stomach. OK, so she was only five feet two, but she'd stood up to that man who hadn't wanted Floella treating him last week and he'd been twice the size of the puny X-ray technician.

Which could only mean that incredibly—inexplicably—she was actually attracted to the creep.

Was she insane? he wondered, risking a quick glance across at her. God in heaven, she could do so much better—deserved so much better—and the thought of her in Jerry

Clark's arms, of him holding her, touching her, making love to her...

'How much longer are you going to be with those damn urine and guiac tests, Flo?' he snapped, taking his anger out in the nearest available person. 'I could have had them flown to America and processed in the time it's taken you to do them!'

The staff nurse blinked, but her voice when she spoke was calm, even. 'There's no blood in the urine, and the guiac and liver function tests are normal, too.'

Without a word he strode through the cubicle curtains, indicating with a jerk of his head that Hannah should follow him.

'You're absolutely certain she's not pregnant?' he demanded the minute they were safely out of Sheila Vernon's earshot. 'Ectopics can cause severe abdominal pain if the foetus is hiding in the liver, or under the bowels, and if the foetus grows into a blood vessel and ruptures it...'

The results could be catastrophic. Massive internal bleeding would occur, and if it wasn't detected in time, a patient could die.

'The blood test was definitely negative,' Hannah assured him.

His frown deepened. 'At twenty-nine she's too young for diverticulitis...inflammation of the colon...'

'What about pelvic inflammatory disease?' Hannah suggested. 'Or endometriosis?'

'It could be,' he murmured. 'But did you notice how swollen her stomach was, and yet she was otherwise quite slim? I think we're looking at a ruptured ovarian cyst here, and I'd like to get the consultant down from Gynae.'

Hannah wasn't about to argue with him. She was much too relieved to have him take charge. But there was something she wanted to say, and she waited until he'd replaced the phone to say it.

'Something wrong?' he asked, seeing she hadn't moved.

She shook her head. 'I just… I only wanted to say thanks for helping me in there.'

'It's what I'm paid for,' he replied dismissively, but as he turned to go she put out her hand to stop him.

'Perhaps it is, but…' She came to a halt. Robert was staring down at her hand on his arm and she withdrew it self-consciously. 'I still… I felt I ought to say thank you, and…' She took a deep breath and met his gaze. 'I'm very sorry about what happened to your wife.'

She had disappeared back into cubicle 2 before he could reply. Which was just as well, he decided as he stared after her because he was too busy wondering why—when he'd gazed down at her small hand on his arm—he'd been seized with the quite bewildering and totally inexplicable desire to grab hold of it and never let go.

It was crazy, ridiculous. She was just a skinny kid with a snub nose and a mop of curly short hair. A skinny kid he heartily wished he could transfer to some other department.

No, he didn't really wish that. She might be relatively naïve and inexperienced at the moment, but in time he knew she could be a real asset to A and E.

And she wasn't really skinny either, he was forced to admit when she reappeared at the cubicle curtains and beckoned to Kelly to join her. She was slender. Slender, but with curves in all the right places. Slender, with a tiny waist, and fine, delicately boned legs. The kind of legs which would wrap themselves around a man, holding him, while he…

'Everything OK, boss?' Jane asked curiously as she passed him.

Hot colour flamed across his cheeks. 'Fine—great.'

But it wasn't fine, and it wasn't great. He didn't want to

find Hannah Blake attractive. He didn't want to find *any* woman attractive, ever again.

And certainly not a woman who could be interested in a jerk like Jerry Clark, he thought grimly as the X-ray technician came through the swing doors with the gynaecological consultant.

'All I can say is this had better be an ovarian cyst and not plain old indigestion, Robert,' the consultant said with a grin. 'I'll have you know I was enjoying coffee with Gorgeous Gussie Granton in Paediatrics—'

'Well, pardon me for interrupting your social life!' Robert snapped as Hannah joined them and he saw Jerry wink across at her. 'I was under the impression this was a hospital, not a dating agency!'

The consultant's smile vanished in an instant. 'Now, just a minute, Robert—'

'I don't have one,' he retorted. 'Unlike you, I have neither time for cups of coffee nor for socialising. I have work to do!'

And before the consultant could reply, he'd walked away, leaving Hannah staring after him in stunned dismay.

Oh, God, but what was he doing? He'd asked the consultant to come down—specifically requested his help—and then to walk out on him...

Awkwardly she cleared her throat, all too aware that the gynaecological consultant was fuming beside her. 'I... We—we're very busy tonight, sir.'

'Are you, indeed?' he replied tightly. 'Well, personally I've never believed that being busy excused rudeness, and I can only hope your boss has acquired a set of better manners by the time I've finished examining his patient!'

He hadn't, not even when it was confirmed that Sheila Vernon was, indeed, suffering from a ruptured ovarian cyst. In fact, at eleven o'clock the whole A and E team sent up a collective prayer of thanks that their shift was over.

'I, for one, hope I don't have to put in another shift like that in a hurry,' Elliot observed ruefully as he accompanied Hannah out of the hospital. 'Talk about stressful!'

'I'd rather not remember it at all,' Hannah sighed, noticing Robert had come out of the hospital, too, and was standing watching them, his face cold and impassive. 'In fact, all I want to do is go home and go to bed.'

Elliot wiggled his eyebrows at her. 'Sounds good to me. Fancy some company?'

She shook her head and laughed. 'I'll see you tomorrow, Elliot.'

'Look, why don't I take you out for dinner?' he pressed. 'Cheer both of us up a bit. I know this really nice little place—' He swore under his breath as his pager suddenly went off. 'No, don't go,' he insisted. 'Give me five minutes to find out if this is urgent, and then at the very least let me take you for coffee.'

She laughed again as he disappeared back into the hospital, but her laughter died when she saw Robert striding across the hospital forecourt towards her, his face even grimmer than before.

'Look, whatever it is, can't it wait until tomorrow?' she said quickly to forestall him. 'I'm really tired—'

'I'm not surprised!' he thundered back, his grey eyes ice-cold. 'First it's Jerry Clark, and now it's Elliot. Frankly, I'm surprised you can find the time to treat any patients when you're so busy organising your social life!'

She stared up at him, open-mouthed. 'I beg your pardon?'

'As well you might, but I'm not here to judge your morals—or, indeed, apparent lack of them!'

'My lack of—'

'My job is to ensure that A and E functions to the best of its ability. A task that is not being made any easier by a junior doctor who seems incapable of resisting the temptation to flirt with anything in trousers!'

It was the injustice of his remark that cut her to the quick. She didn't have a social life, not after working an eight-hour shift each day then going home to study for her exams. And for him to suggest she was some sort of raving nymphomaniac...

She gripped her hands together tightly, and when she spoke every word sizzled like hot oil. 'I don't know why I should even dignify your comments with an answer, but for your information I think Jerry Clark is a creep.'

'A creep whose attentions you don't appear to find particularly distasteful!'

'Only because I can't afford to!' she retorted. 'If you were a woman doctor at St Stephen's, you'd know that if you want your X-rays processed quickly you have to put up with Jerry's crude innuendoes, and touching, and pawing.'

He looked truly horrified. 'That's sexual harassment—'

'Too damn right it is, so think yourself lucky you don't wear a skirt and have to endure it!'

'Hannah—'

'And as for your suggestion that I flirt with Elliot!' She dug her fingernails deep into the palms of her hands and struggled to keep calm. 'I talk to him. I laugh with him. It's called making conversation with friends, Dr Cunningham. Something you quite obviously neither recognise nor subscribe to, so I'm not surprised you haven't got any!'

He whitened then reddened in quick succession. Never had she seen him quite so angry, but to her dismay there wasn't just anger in his face but pain, too. Conscience-stricken, she took a step towards him. 'Dr Cunningham... Robert...'

He didn't even wait to hear what she'd been about to

say. He simply wheeled round and strode away, and she bit her lip when she heard Elliot's deep groan behind her.

'I went too far, didn't I?' she mumbled unhappily, turning towards him.

'The words "a little" and "over the top" certainly spring to mind,' he said with a sigh. 'I don't know what it is with you two. Five minutes together, and you're at each other's throats.'

He was right. She wasn't normally so quick to anger—in fact, it was usually quite the reverse. Only her father had ever managed to rile her quite so much, and she didn't want to think about her father, not tonight, not ever.

'I've got to go, Elliot.'

'But what about dinner—coffee?' he protested.

'Maybe some other night,' she said gently, seeing his disappointment. 'Look, I wouldn't be good company—not for anyone.'

He nodded reluctantly, but as she began to walk away he suddenly came after her. 'Hannah, about Robert...'

'What about Robert?' she demanded.

'Apologise to him. Look, it doesn't matter who was at fault,' he added when she opened her mouth to protest. 'You've got to work with the guy, and...well...I know it's no excuse, but today—with it being the anniversary of his wife's death—it must have been really hellish for him.'

Elliot was right. It didn't excuse what Robert had said to her tonight, but it might explain it, a little.

And if she was going to apologise she might as well do it now, she decided, hitching her bag higher onto her shoulder. Wellington Place was only a couple of streets away. A quick detour on her way home and it would be done.

Or at least it would have been if she hadn't arrived in Wellington Place to find Robert's ground-floor flat in total darkness. Either he'd gone out, or gone to bed, and it didn't require the brains of Einstein to figure out he wouldn't exactly be thrilled if she woke him up simply to say she was sorry.

With a sigh she began retracing her steps, only to come to a sudden halt. From somewhere inside the flat she was sure she'd heard the sound of breaking glass. Could he be ill? Could he have collapsed? Could he be so eaten up with grief that he'd done something really stupid?

She ran back to the front door, put her finger on the doorbell and kept it there. Five minutes. She'd give him five minutes to answer, and if he didn't—

'Will you get your damn finger off that bloody doorbell before you wake the whole neighbourhood?'

Robert wasn't ill, she realised with dismay as she gazed up into his furious face. He was angry. Angry at being disturbed, angry with her for being there, and then suddenly she noticed something else. Blood was trickling down from his wrist onto his shirt cuff, staining it black under the fluorescent streetlight.

'Oh, my God, what have you done?' she gasped in horror.

'Done?' he repeated blankly.

'Your wrist... Have you any SteriStrips—antiseptic—in the house?' she asked, pushing past him into the flat. 'I'll need water, towels, too. Oh, Robert, I know you're upset—unhappy—but to do something like this...'

'Something like what?' he protested in obvious confusion as he followed her. 'I simply tripped and fell when I was carrying some glasses, and some of the glass went into my wrist and arm.'

'Then you didn't— I mean, you weren't trying to...' She coloured furiously under his puzzled gaze. 'Look, where's your bathroom?'

'Over there, but—'

'You'd better take off your shirt,' she ordered, slipping off her coat and throwing it over the chair in the hall as she led the way into the bathroom. 'If you've cut your arm as well as your wrist, they're both going to need attention. Lacerations can cause infection—'

'Hannah—'

'What on earth were you doing, stumbling about in the dark in the first place?' she demanded, taking refuge in anger when what she really felt was acute embarrassment at having so clearly jumped to the wrong conclusion. 'Saving on electricity—checking your night sight?'

'Hannah—'

'And as for this little lot,' she continued, shaking her head in disbelief when she opened his bathroom cabinet and scanned its contents, 'most of this—'

'Should have been thrown out years ago. Yeah, I know.' A rueful smile curved his lips as she turned angrily towards him, then appeared to forget what she'd been about to say. 'There's no need to look quite so shocked, little Hannah. The whisky's purely for medicinal purposes.'

It wasn't the glass of whisky in his hand that had made her bereft her of speech—though, heaven knows, he should have known better. It was the sight of his bare, broad, muscular chest. A bare, broad, muscular chest covered with an intriguing pattern of glistening dark hair. A bare, broad, muscular chest which for some inexplicable reason seemed to be doing the most amazing things to her heart rate

'I...um... You don't appear to have any sterile dressings,' she spluttered, swinging back to his bathroom cabinet. 'I...I'll have to make do with lint and Micropore.'

'Whatever,' he said dismissively. 'But could you get a move on before I freeze to death?'

He was lucky, she thought, letting out her breath in a rush. Hot flushes were her problem at the moment. Mega-hot flushes.

And it was crazy, ridiculous. This man was her boss. She'd worked with him for over a month and never once thought of him as a man. OK, so when he'd smiled at her that one time, she might have thought he had a very nice smile, but she'd never thought of him as A Man. And yet now...

Now she was all too aware of him. All too aware of the rapid rise and fall of his chest, and her own skittering heartbeat.

'Could you...?' Her voice had come out in a squeak, and she took a firm grip on herself. 'Could you sit down on the edge of the bath for me, please?'

He nodded absently, but a frown creased his forehead when she began cleaning his arm with some lint. 'Forgive my appalling memory, but did I actually invite you round here tonight?'

The colour on her cheeks darkened to crimson. 'I came to apologise. I was very rude to you earlier—'

'Water off a duck's back,' he interrupted dismissively, wincing slightly as she dabbed at his wrist and arm with antiseptic. 'If everyone I'd been rude to during the day came round to my flat to apologise, there'd be a queue stretching back to St Stephen's.'

There probably would be, she thought wryly, leaning over him to retrieve the Micropore. 'OK, I think I've got all the glass out, but I'm afraid your arm and wrist are going to be pretty sore tomorrow.'

They were pretty sore right now, but that wasn't what was making him twist uncomfortably on the edge of the bath. It was the feel of her warm breath against his throat as she bent over him, the caress of her hair against his cheek as she tilted her head in concentration.

God in heaven, what was the matter with him? he wondered, gritting his teeth as he felt his body unmistakably stirring in response. He scarcely knew this girl. His traitorous body shouldn't be responding to the rapid rise and fall of her small, high breasts. His hands shouldn't be trembling with the urge to reach for her, to slide her onto his lap, to...

'I really don't think you should drink any of that,' Hannah protested as he reached for his glass of whisky and took a gulp from it.

She was right, he shouldn't, but because he didn't know how to deal with the conflicting emotions her nearness was provoking, he took refuge in the simplest—anger.

'What I choose to drink is none of your damn business!' he retorted, getting to his feet so abruptly that she banged back against the bath.

'I know it isn't, Robert, but drinking isn't going to solve anything. I know about your wife—'

'You know *nothing* about my wife!' he roared, making her jump. 'What do you know about love, and loss, and heartache? Little Miss Muffet with your big brown eyes and bouncing curls. Little Miss Muffet who's probably never been properly kissed by a man, far less been made love to by one!'

Hot colour flooded her cheeks. He was wrong, but she wasn't about to tell him about Chris. She wasn't about to tell him anything.

'I think I'd better go.'

'Running away, Miss Muffet?' he mocked.

'Will you please stop calling me that?' she protested.

'But that's what you are,' he said, his voice brutal, biting. 'Little Miss Muffet, who thinks she has the answer to everything. Little Miss Muffet without a care in the world.' He leant towards her, his gaze suddenly sharp. 'But you do have a care, don't you? Or more precisely a secret. What's your deep dark secret, Hannah? Come on, let's trade. I'll tell you why I fully intend to get blind drunk tonight, and you can tell me what made you leave Edinburgh.'

She stared up at him silently. She wished she hadn't come. She wished she'd waited until morning to apologise like any other sensible person. But most of all she wished she didn't feel the quite ridiculous urge to reach out, take him in her arms and somehow comfort him.

Quickly she retrieved her handbag. 'I think I should go home.'

'Go on, then—run away!' Robert jeered, and she would have done if the bathroom hadn't been so small, and he hadn't been so big, and she hadn't tripped in her haste to get past him.

And he would have let her go if she hadn't stumbled straight into his arms and the touch of her hands on his bare chest hadn't sent a jolt through his body like lightning.

For a second he froze. Let her go, his mind urged, get her out of the house, but his body wasn't listening to his mind. His body wanted her. Wanted to bury itself in her soft sweetness, and forget at least for a time the bleak emptiness that lay inside him. And he surrendered to those demands.

His lips came down on hers with a bruising intensity, his arms crushed her to him, and a groan escaped him as he felt her small high breasts against his chest, a groan of desperate, desolate need.

God, but he wanted her, wanted her so much. His head was spinning with desire as he covered her face and throat with searing kisses. His body was hard, aching, desperate for release as he slid his hands up her sides to cup her breasts, and the result would have been inevitable if the wailing sound of an ambulance siren in the street outside hadn't suddenly penetrated his brain and brought him to his senses.

What was he doing? he wondered as he shuddered and drew back from her to stare with inward horror at her flushed face, her swollen lips and dazed eyes.

'I'm sorry,' he muttered thickly. 'So sorry. What I just did… Unforgivable… Completely unforgivable—'

'Robert—'

Her eyes were dark, confused, bewildered, and jerkily he grabbed her by the elbow, thrust her coat and bag into her arms and propelled her to the front door. 'Go home, Hannah. Go home now.'

'But, Robert—'

He couldn't bear to hear any more. Couldn't bear to even look at her and realise what he'd almost done. With a muttered oath he shut the door, and leant his forehead against it, and heartily wished that he'd never been born.

CHAPTER FOUR

'I CAN quite understand why you thought he might have gallstones,' Robert observed as he accompanied Hannah out of the cubicle. 'The acute pain in his upper abdomen, his extreme pallor and nausea—'

'And all he's got is plain, old-fashioned indigestion,' she interrupted, completely mortified.

'Stomach pain is one of the hardest things to diagnose, Hannah,' he said gently. 'There can be so many reasons behind it, and I did advise you to always think the worst. Just remember in future not to become so convinced you've got a zebra that you forget all about the donkeys.'

'The donkeys?' she repeated, puzzled, and he smiled.

'It's something one of my old professors used to say. In medicine we can all too easily become so hung up on our own knowledge that we can forget the commonplace, and go looking instead for the exotic.'

'And you certainly can't get much more commonplace than dyspepsia,' she sighed ruefully. 'I feel like such an idiot.'

'Don't. It might well have been gallstones, and you were right to ask for a second opinion.'

She nodded without conviction. 'Thanks for helping, and I'll remember what you said about the donkeys and zebras.'

He smiled again, and she fully expected him to go, but to her surprise he didn't.

'It's very quiet in here today,' he observed, glancing round the treatment room.

She supposed it was if you considered thirty patients still waiting out in Reception a quiet day.

'In fact,' Robert continued, 'for a Thursday, it's quite amazingly quiet.'

He glanced down at his watch, adjusted his name tag, then to her acute dismay he cleared his throat awkwardly.

Oh, no, he was going to talk about what had happened in his flat. He was obviously trying to get up the nerve to do it, and it was the last thing she wanted. What could she possibly say in reply? Forget it? It meant nothing? Men are always kissing me?

'Hannah—'

'Did you hear about the homeless man I sent up to ward 12—the one with the gangrenous leg?' she said, beginning to edge casually away. 'They had to amputate eventually.'

'Did they?' he murmured, following her.

She nodded. 'I don't know how he's going to manage. Life on the streets is hard enough for someone fit and healthy, but for a man with one leg...'

'If you're really worried about him, why don't you contact the hospital social services department?' he asked. 'They might be able to find him hostel accommodation, though I've got to say that many men who've lived rough for years can't bear to have a roof over their heads. They feel shut in, trapped.'

'Do they?' She risked a quick glance up at him, decided it was a very bad idea and transferred her gaze to his shirt buttons instead.

'Hannah—'

'I didn't know so many people slept rough until I came to London,' she told the shirt buttons, knowing perfectly well that she was babbling but wishing only that he would go away. 'We have homeless people back in Edinburgh, but nothing on this scale.'

'I suppose not. Hannah—'

'It might be quieter today than normal, but there are still

quite a few people waiting to be seen, and I really should—'

'Get back to work,' Robert finished for her, his voice oddly flat.

Idiot, her mind whispered as she peeped over her shoulder in time to see him disappearing into the office. He probably hadn't even been going to talk to you about what happened in his flat at all, and now he thinks you're some sort of lamebrain half-wit. Good grief, it happened three days ago, and as he hasn't even hinted about it before, the likelihood of him doing so now—in the middle of the treatment room—is pretty remote. In fact, considering he told you that he had every intention of getting blind drunk, he probably doesn't even remember.

But she remembered.

Oh, yes, she remembered. Remembered the bruising intensity of his kisses. Remembered how her initial surprise had quickly given way to desire. How she'd wanted him to keep on touching her with those unbelievable hands, to satisfy a hunger she hadn't even known she'd possessed.

And it was crazy. She couldn't possibly be attracted to Robert Cunningham. No woman in her right mind could possibly be attracted to a man who in the space of five short weeks had ignored her, clucked round her like a manic broody hen, then suddenly kissed her with a desperation that had taken her breath away.

No, she wasn't attracted to him, she told herself firmly. She felt sorry for him—who wouldn't? And that night she'd been a bit low herself. Low, and a little bit lonely, and as for Robert...

He'd been lonely, too, grieving for his dead wife, and his solution to his loneliness had been sex. Sex with anyone, and she'd just happened to be there, available. She mustn't read any more into it than that. If she did she'd only be hurt again, and that was the last thing she wanted.

'You seem a bit preoccupied this afternoon, Hannah,' Jane observed after they'd arranged for a porter to take the elderly man in cubicle 4, who had fractured his forearm, to the plastering department. 'Something troubling you?'

'I was just thinking about Elliot,' she lied, gesturing towards the SHO who was quite mercilessly teasing their student nurse.

'Dangerous occupation, that,' the sister declared, her grey eyes sparkling. 'Thinking about Elliot.'

'I know.' Hannah laughed. 'And there's no need for you to get worried. I mean, I like him—I do—but...'

Jane rolled her grey eyes expressively and nodded. 'It's an awfully big but, isn't it?'

'Do you think he'll ever settle down with just one girl?' Hannah asked.

'Not a hope, I'm afraid. The trouble with Elliot—though you'd never ever get him to admit it—is that with one failed marriage behind him he's terrified of being hurt again and so he simply flits from girl to girl. Some men are like that. Others, like Robert, fall in love once, and can't ever fall in love again.'

'Can't they?' Hannah said, wondering why she should find that opinion so deeply depressing.

Jane shook her head. 'It's quite sad, really. Robert was never a great lady's man—in fact, we all thought he was married to his work—but when Laura joined the department he fell for her, hook, line and sinker. Mind you, so did every other red-blooded male in the hospital,' she added with a chuckle.

'She was very pretty, then?' Hannah murmured, her eyes following Robert as he came out of the office.

'And how. Think Marilyn Monroe but with red hair. And clever! Boy, was Laura clever. Top grades at med school, a gold medal prizewinner in obstetrics and physiology. She was consultant material for sure.'

Hannah sighed inwardly. Nobody had ever said she was consultant material. Nobody had ever said she looked like Marilyn Monroe either—with or without red hair. Minnie Mouse perhaps, but not Marilyn Monroe.

'Jane—'

'If that's Admin on the phone again about those requisition forms, I swear I'll rip the damn thing off the wall,' the sister groaned as the phone in the treatment room began to ring. 'Honestly, Hannah, you'd think we had nothing better to do with our time than fill in bits of paper!'

Hannah laughed, but she felt anything but amused later that afternoon when Elliot caught her by the arm and hustled her to the side of the treatment room after she'd finished treating a young girl with a dislocated shoulder.

'Elliot, this had better be important,' she protested as he gazed down at her, his blue eyes gleaming. 'The waiting room's filling up again—'

'And I've just realised I'm an idiot!' he exclaimed.

'I thought Jane had already told you that,' she responded, torn between irritation and amusement. 'In fact—'

'I should have recognised your name immediately,' he continued. 'Charles Blake, the eminent Edinburgh gynaecologist. Charles Blake, whose wife Hannah tragically died in childbirth. Hannah, you're *Charles Blake's* daughter!'

'Elliot, will you keep your voice down?' she cried, glancing nervously round in case anyone had heard him.

'But your father's written more award-winning books on gynaecology than I've had hot dinners! He's a legend in his own lifetime. He's—'

'Absolutely wonderful,' she finished for him tightly. 'Yes, I know. And I'm just his plain, ordinary daughter instead of the brilliant, prizewinning son he always wanted.'

Elliot gazed at her uncertainly. 'Hannah, you're not plain, and you're anything but ordinary—'

'Yeah, right,' she said cynically. 'So what are you wanting? An autographed copy of my father's latest book—an introduction to him?'

'I don't want anything,' he protested. 'Look, I'm sorry if I've upset you—'

'Of course you haven't upset me,' she said with spurious brightness. 'Why should I be upset because you admire my father? Everyone admires my father.'

Including Chris, she remembered with an unwanted shaft of pain. Chris who'd said he loved her, and she'd believed him, until she'd found out he'd only wanted to marry her to fast-track his own medical career.

'Hannah—'

'Please, don't tell anyone about my father,' she begged. 'I know everyone will find out eventually, but—'

'What do you take me for?' Elliot exclaimed, clearly deeply hurt by her suggestion. 'Of course I won't tell anyone.'

'Thank you,' she murmured, but as she turned to go he touched her arm sympathetically. 'Hannah, love… I'm really sorry. I thought…well, I assumed you'd be thrilled to bits, so proud—'

'So does everyone,' she said with a slightly crooked smile, and neither of them noticed Robert watching them from across the room, his eyes bleak, his hands bunched tightly by his sides.

Why had he done it? Why had he kissed her? Even now he could neither understand nor explain his behaviour. OK, so he'd been deeply unhappy, remembering the good times he and Laura had shared before it had all gone disastrously wrong, but if that ambulance hadn't gone by, if its wailing siren hadn't brought him to his senses…

He closed his eyes tightly. What must Hannah think of him? All too vividly he could remember the concern in her deep brown eyes, her belief, he now realised, that he'd been attempting to slash his wrists. And how had he repaid her kindness?

He wanted to apologise to her again. He desperately wanted to apologise again, but what good would it do? She was already tiptoeing around him, clearly deeply uncomfortable in his presence. Better by far that she believed he couldn't remember what had happened than resurrect an incident she so obviously longed to forget.

But he remembered.

Yes, he remembered all too vividly the feel of her body against his. Her tiny waist, so small his hands could span it, the gentle curve of her breasts, surprisingly full under his fingers, and the odd little cry she'd given when he'd crushed her to him—the cry he'd echoed with a groan, wanting her, wanting her so much.

His lips twisted bitterly. Wanted, not loved. Lust. An old-fashioned word, but an accurate one, he thought as he gazed across at her, and felt his groin tighten as he saw her smile at something Elliot had said. And as an adult, mature male he had to deal with it, conquer it.

But that didn't mean he had to stand by and watch Elliot talking to her so intimately, he decided, striding grimly across the treatment room before he had time to rationalise his thoughts.

'Care to tell me what's so important that it's had your heads together for the past ten minutes while we have patients waiting?' he demanded, his eyes flicking coldly from Elliot to Hannah.

'I...um... It wasn't really that important,' Hannah muttered, all too aware that the blush she could feel creeping across her cheeks suggested otherwise.

'Then if you've both finished whatever world-shattering topic you've been discussing,' Robert snapped, 'I suggest you get yourselves back to work!'

And with that he strode away, leaving Hannah staring unhappily after him.

'I really seem to have the knack of making him angry, don't I?' She sighed.

'He's not angry with you, love,' Elliot said thoughtfully. 'Maybe *about* you, but not *at* you.'

'You mean, he heard what we were talking about?' she said with dismay.

He shook his head. 'If Robert had heard you admitting to being Charles Blake's daughter, half of London would have heard his roar.'

'But he doesn't know my father—'

'He doesn't need to. Robert's parents had to make a lot of sacrifices to put him through med school, and he's got no time for the children of rich consultants pulling strings to get posts.'

'But I didn't pull any strings,' she protested. 'My father doesn't even know where I'm working.'

'Really?' Elliot exclaimed in surprise. 'But surely—'

'I'm sorry, Elliot,' she interrupted quickly, though in truth she wasn't one bit sorry to put a stop to a conversation she would far rather not have had. 'I have to go. Jane seems to want me.'

And she did. Calm, implacable Jane, who never flapped, was in a flap now.

'What is it—what's wrong?' Hannah asked as she joined her outside cubicle 7.

'John Keir, forty two years old, came in ten minutes ago with severe chest pains, and I'm not happy.'

Neither was Hannah after she'd examined him. John Keir's pulse was 145, his breathing was rapid, and his skin was warm and clammy to the touch.

'How long have you felt like this, Mr Keir?' she asked.

'A couple of hours,' he gasped. 'Maybe more. At first I thought it was simply indigestion. Some friends and I went out for a pub lunch, you see, but now it feels like I've got an elephant sitting on my chest.'

'Do you have pain anywhere else?' Hannah said as Jane swiftly began inserting an IV drip.

'It's down my left arm now as well,' he replied with difficulty, 'and in my jaw.'

Hannah eyes met Jane's. Mr Keir couldn't have described the classic symptoms of a heart attack better if he'd tried.

'Get me a BP and respiratory rate, Jane,' she said, pulling the ECG monitor quickly across to the trolley.

'You'll be wanting supplementary oxygen, too?' Jane said, reaching for the nasal cannula.

Hannah nodded as she began affixing the ECG machine's sticky electrodes to John Keir's arms, legs and chest. The extra oxygen should help the man's breathing and hopefully bring his blood pressure down. A nitroglycerine capsule under his tongue, and morphine given intravenously, should relieve his pain, but they needed to know what his heart was doing, and only the ECG machine could tell them that.

And it did. Myocardial infarction. The horizontal lines appearing at regular intervals on the graph paper could mean only one thing—acute myocardial infarction.

'Resps 130 over 90, breaths 24 a minute,' Jane murmured, and Hannah bit her lip. This was far too serious for her to handle on her own, and she knew it.

'Jane, go and see if you can find Elliot or Robert,' she said in an undertone, 'and I want you to page Cardiology for me, too.'

'But—'

'Just do it, Jane,' she insisted.

With a backward glance of concern the sister was gone, and Hannah smiled encouragingly down at John Keir as she inserted another IV line into his arm.

'You said you went out for a pub lunch,' she commented,

deliberately making conversation to calm him. 'Somewhere nice?'

'The Arches in Piccadilly,' he replied with a wobbly smile. 'Last time I'll be going there, believe me. One tomato risotto with avocado, followed by lamb steaks cooked in sage butter, and I end up in hospital.'

Hannah chuckled, understanding the effort it must have taken John Keir to make a joke at a time like this, then glanced up at the drip. It was open and running and hopefully it would soon dilate the arteries around John's heart, helping the blood to flow more freely and making it less likely to form clots.

Unfortunately, none of the drugs she'd given him through the IV drip could unclog any clots already present. Only tissue-plasminogen activating factor and streptokinase could do that, but even healthy people without heart problems could sometimes bleed too much when they were given those two drugs, and the thought of John Keir bleeding internally, as well as suffering from a myocardial infarction, horrified her

She needed advice, and she needed it quickly. As though on cue, Jane suddenly came through the cubicle curtains with Robert at her side.

'Drug situation?' he declared, pulling on a pair of latex gloves.

'Nitroglycerine by mouth, morphine intravenously. Nitro drip with heparin and aspirin,' Hannah replied.

'TPA and streptokinase?'

She shook her head. 'I wasn't sure about the dosages—'

'No problem,' he interrupted.

With an ease she could only envy, he swiftly made the calculations and administered the two drugs. They should work quickly, and they did.

'BP and pulse rate seem to be stabilising, Robert,' Jane announced.

'OK, page IC for me, Jane. Tell them we'll be sending Mr...Mr...'

'Keir—John Keir,' Hannah supplied for him.

'A Mr John Keir along after he's been seen by the cardiology specialist. Hannah, keep an eye on the ECG monitor for arrhythmia—abnormal heartbeats.'

She nodded. 'Do you want—?'

She didn't get a chance to say any more. The alarm on the ECG machine suddenly went off and she stared at it in horror.

Ventricular fibrillation. John Keir's heart had gone into chaotic, uncoordinated spasm. No blood was flowing from his heart into his brain, which meant that he would soon be dead unless they did something. But to Hannah's dismay she couldn't move, couldn't even think. All she could feel was panic—a terrified, mind-numbing, panic—and desperately she glanced across at Robert, willing him to do something.

He did. He leant past her and thumped John Keir hard in the centre of his chest with his fist. Hannah's eyes flew back to the ECG monitor. Nothing. Nothing was happening. The graph paper was still spewing out the same wild, haphazard strokes, then with a discordant beep the alarm suddenly clicked off, and John Keir's heart rhythm jolted back to normal.

'Sorry about that.' Robert smiled as John Keir gazed up at him in confusion. 'Hitting somebody isn't exactly the best way to win friends, but sometimes it can be very effective.' He glanced across at Jane. 'BP now?'

'One hundred over sixty.'

Normal, considering the circumstances.

'Any sign of arrhythmia, Hannah?' he asked.

'No,' she mumbled.

Robert shot her a puzzled glance, but she didn't see it. All she could think was that John Keir's blood pressure was normal. He wasn't out of the woods yet by any means, but for now, at least, he was stable again.

'Where the hell is that cardiology consultant?' Robert demanded. 'You did say you'd paged him, didn't you, Jane?'

She nodded. 'He said he was on his way.'

'Don't tell me I've missed all the excitement,' the consultant said as he swung into the cubicle.

'I sincerely hope so,' Robert replied dryly. 'I think Mr Keir's had more than enough for one afternoon.'

So had she, Hannah thought as John Keir was wheeled off to Intensive Care. She'd had more than enough to last her a lifetime.

A sob sprang to her lips and she crushed it down with difficulty. She'd failed. This had been her first big emergency, and she'd failed.

'Are you OK, Hannah?'

She glanced over her shoulder to see Robert gazing at her with concern, and shook her head. 'I don't ever want to be that frightened again as long as I live. If you hadn't been here—done what you did—'

'It comes with practice.'

'He could have died,' she continued, her eyes large brown pools of distress and defeat. 'I just stood there— useless—frozen—'

'Hannah, nobody expects a junior doctor to have the knowledge and skill of a special registrar,' he protested.

Perhaps not, but she'd bet money Laura wouldn't have frozen. In fact, Laura would probably have performed open-heart surgery with a teaspoon if she'd needed to.

'I'm useless,' she murmured wretchedly. 'Completely useless—'

'Hey, you can stop that right now!' Robert exclaimed, striding quickly across the cubicle and grasping her firmly by the shoulders. 'Who gave that guy the nitro, heparin and aspirin? *You* did! Who had the sense to get help when she needed it? *You* did!'

'Yes, but—'

'Hannah, you did everything I—or indeed anyone else—could have expected in the circumstances, so why are you being so hard on yourself?'

Because for years my father told me I'd never be good enough to be a doctor, she thought. For years I had to listen to him telling me I wasn't bright enough, or strong enough, or talented enough.

'I guess…' Her tears were still far too near to the surface for comfort, and she swallowed hard. 'I guess it's because I'm a wimp.'

He smiled. A gentle smile that seemed to curl down right into her toes. 'Oh, Hannah, you're not a wimp. You might be an idiot at times, but you're most definitely not a wimp.'

She gave a short, hiccuping laugh that wasn't quite a sob. 'Am I supposed to take that as a compliment?'

'It's meant as one.' He nodded, and she knew he wasn't lying.

But as she continued to gaze up at him she suddenly realised something else. The strange, fluttery sensation in the pit of her stomach was back again. That confusing, disturbing, awareness she'd experienced in his flat had returned, and she didn't want to feel it. She desperately didn't want to feel it.

Awkwardly she backed away from him, all too conscious that her cheeks must be red. 'I have to get back to work. Jane…Elliot…they'll be wondering where I am.'

'Hannah…' Robert took a step towards her, then stopped. 'If you ever feel the need to talk to someone, perhaps feel that things—people—are getting on top of you…'

She wished he hadn't said that. He'd been the last person to be on top of her, well, almost, and she didn't want to remember that. Didn't want to remember the way he'd kissed her, how his fingers had curled round her breasts, and how he'd pressed his long, hard length against her.

'I'll...I'll bear that in mind,' she floundered, backing away from him still further.

'Hannah—'

'Oh, I'm sorry,' Elliot said, abruptly halting as he came through the cubicle curtains. 'I didn't realise you were busy, Robert, but the night staff have just come on duty—'

'And I'm just going,' Hannah broke in quickly.

'Hannah, wait a minute—'

But she didn't wait. She simply took to her heels and ran.

Idiot. *Idiot!* she berated herself when she reached the staffroom and leant against the door, her heart pounding. Are you deliberately trying to make yourself look ridiculous? Deliberately trying to look a fool? Look at the situation. Yes, just *look*!

Robert was married to a girl who was beautiful, and talented, and smart. Even if he wanted to get involved with somebody again, it wouldn't be with somebody like you.

And even if he was interested in you, you swore you'd never ever get involved with another doctor again, remember, so get a grip on yourself. Go home, have something to eat, and then you'll be able to get this whole ridiculous situation into perspective.

And the hot meal did help. The long, hot shower she took afterwards helped even more.

You've got to start socialising, she told herself as she stepped out of the shower, slipped into her bathrobe and went through to the sitting room to collect her hairdryer. You go to work, come home, then study. No wonder you're behaving like an idiot. If you don't get yourself a social life pretty damn quick, you're going to start finding creepy Jerry Clark from Radiology attractive next.

She chuckled, switched on the dryer, then switched it off

again when she heard the sound of someone knocking on her door.

It would be Melanie Johnson from the flat above, dropping by to collect the notes she'd wanted to borrow. Melanie, who was scatty and crazy and exactly the kind of company she needed right now. With a smile she called out, 'Come in. The door's not locked.'

Which would have been exactly the right thing to say if it had been Melanie, but it wasn't. It was Robert Cunningham.

For a second she froze, all too acutely aware that she was naked beneath her bathrobe, then with a deep blush of embarrassment she dropped the hairdryer, grabbed the belt of her robe and tightened it into a firm knot.

'I thought...I thought you were Melanie,' she said, in case he thought she made a habit of asking people into her flat when she was wearing a bathrobe. 'Melanie Johnson,' she added as his eyebrows rose. 'She has the flat above me, and wanted to borrow some of my notes on blood diseases. She had flu when we had the lecture, you see, and...and...'

And she was babbling, she realised as he gazed at her silently. Babbling a lot of nonsense that he couldn't possibly be interested in.

Well, what did he expect? she thought crossly. She hadn't asked him to drop by, she hadn't wanted him to drop by, and if he wanted scintillating conversation he'd come to the wrong place.

'What can I do for you?' she asked as coolly as any girl dressed solely in a wet bathrobe, with bright red cheeks and soaking wet hair, could be expected to. 'Is there some problem at the hospital?'

'No problem, no,' he replied. 'Reception told me that a letter came for you this morning marked ''personal'', and I thought it might be important.'

In truth, he hadn't thought anything of the kind. He'd

come because he still felt guilty, because she'd seemed so depressed over John Keir, and when he'd seen the letter he'd hoped it might be from a friend who could cheer her up, but the minute he'd walked into her flat he'd known he shouldn't have come.

Did she have any idea how revealing her bathrobe was when it was wet? He knew, and wished he didn't, and with a supreme effort of will he shifted his gaze to her face and kept it there.

'Thanks for bringing it round,' she murmured, taking the letter from his outstretched hand.

She didn't looked grateful. In fact, she looked as though he'd just handed her a ticking time bomb to hold.

'Is there something wrong?' he said curiously.

'Of course not,' she replied brightly, shoving the letter into her pocket. 'It's just a letter from an old schoolfriend, that's all.'

And I'm Santa Claus, Robert thought grimly as he stared at her.

How could he have been so stupid? It was obvious now that the letter was from a boyfriend, or a lover. Probably the same lover or boyfriend who'd brought her rushing down to London to work, and, judging from her expression, a letter was the last thing she'd expected.

Well, when you fell in love you got hurt. Everybody knew that. Look at Elliot, divorced now for five years and still unable to form a lasting relationship. And as for himself...

No, he didn't want to think about himself. Didn't want to remember how loving Laura had brought heartbreak and disaster to them both. Quickly he glanced round the sitting room, looking for a way to change the subject. 'These flats are even worse than I remember.'

'You remember?' she repeated.

'My...my wife had one of these flats before...before we

got married.' So much for trying not to remember, he thought bleakly. So much for trying to forget. Nothing would ever help him to forget. Nothing.

'Would you like a cup of coffee, or tea?' she said swiftly, guessing at the thoughts which must be going through his mind. 'It would be no trouble...'

'Thank you, but I have to go.' Robert walked towards the door, then paused and turned back towards her, his face determined. 'I never...I didn't ever thank you properly for taking care of my arm and wrist.'

Hannah gazed at him in dismay. She didn't want to talk about this, not right now and preferably never. 'It was no trouble—no trouble at all,' she replied hurriedly. 'I was only too happy to be there.' Oh, she hadn't meant that— or at least she had, but not in the way he might think. 'What I mean is—'

'I know what you mean,' he interrupted, and she wondered if her cheeks were as red as his. They certainly felt like it. 'I just...well, I wanted to say thank you, and...' A small muscle in the corner of his jaw tightened. 'And to say that I hope I didn't... That is, my behaviour—'

'There's no need to say anything,' she declared, her voice slightly strangled. 'In fact, I'd far rather you didn't.'

He nodded, but he didn't move, made no attempt to open the door. Oh, please, just go, she thought. You've done what you came to do so, please, please, just go.

'I'll say goodnight, then,' he said at last, hesitantly, almost she thought reluctantly, and this time she didn't try to stop him.

Instead, she waited until she heard the sound of his footsteps growing fainter and fainter in the corridor outside, then let out her breath in a long, slow whoosh of relief.

She never wanted to have another conversation like that as long as she lived. He'd been so clearly deeply embarrassed, and she…! If he'd only left that stupid letter until morning—

The letter. Quickly she pulled it out of her pocket and stared down at it.

How had her father found out where she worked? She'd told no one, refused even to so much as give him a hint, so how had he found out? Probably by phoning every hospital in the country, looking for her, she decided bitterly. Probably by calling in every favour he was owed.

Well, she wasn't going to read it now. She didn't know if she was ever going to read it. Deliberately, she threw the envelope onto the coffee-table, switched on her hairdryer and went over to the mirror, only to stare at herself in appalled horror.

Oh, no, she could see the outline of her breasts, even her nipples, through her wet bathrobe, and if she could see them that meant Robert must have seen them, too.

So what if he did? her mind protested. Considering the man was married to a woman whose figure would have made Marilyn Monroe envious, your two poached eggs are hardly likely to have taken his breath away.

And they *were* poached eggs, she thought vexedly, turning sideways to gaze at them critically. Two small, flat, unsexy, poached eggs. If only they were bigger, fuller, higher—

'Oh, for God's sake, get a grip,' she told her reflection. 'Even if you had breasts the size of melons, Robert Cunningham wouldn't be interested in you, and that's exactly how you want it to be, you know it is.'

And as she switched on her hairdryer and began drying her hair, she tried very hard to make herself believe it.

CHAPTER FIVE

'I'M AFRAID your eye is going to be very painful for quite some time,' Hannah said as she slipped an eye patch carefully round the young man's head. 'The antibiotic eye drops I've given you should help a little, and they ought to get rid of any infection, but don't forget to give this referral note to our receptionist on your way out, and she'll make sure you get an appointment at our ophthalmology clinic.'

''Strewth, but I look like Long John Silver,' the man exclaimed with dismay as he got off the trolley and looked at himself in the mirror.

'Be grateful you'll eventually be able to see out of that eye,' Hannah replied. 'Riding a motorbike without goggles might be considered macho but, believe me, losing your eyesight isn't.'

'Yeah, right. Thanks for your time, Doc,' he replied, zipping up his leather jacket. 'And I'll remember what you said about the goggles.'

She doubted it. He'd probably be out on his motorbike in a couple of days, still not wearing his goggles, and end up back in A and E with something considerably more serious.

Cynic, her mind whispered. Too damn right I'm cynical, she thought. Cynical, and jaded, and depressed.

She was so tired, that was the trouble. Not just physically tired—that she thought she could have coped with—but mind-numbingly, brain-sappingly tired, and yet she'd only just come on duty. Only just arrived for the start of the night shift with another eight long weary hours to go.

How did Robert, and Elliot, and Jane work here day after

day, night after night? Where did they get their inner resources from, or had her father been right all the time when he'd said she didn't have the temperament to become a doctor?

She'd thought he'd been wrong. She'd been determined to prove him wrong, but now... Now, she honestly didn't know any more.

'Ah, Hannah, my dear!' Mr Mackay, the consultant in charge of A and E beamed as he breezed down the treatment room towards her, with Robert at his side. 'I need your opinion on the patient in cubicle 1. Woman in her mid-fifties, brought in by her husband because of excruciating pain in the upper left quadrant of her stomach. She was sick after dinner tonight, and brought up some blood.'

Opinion be damned, she thought wearily as she stared up at the consultant's cheery face. Mr Mackay had plainly just realised she'd been with them now for over two months and he was trying to find out whether she was up to scratch or not.

The symptoms he'd outlined indicated that his patient might be suffering from a bleeding stomach ulcer. It probably was a bleeding ulcer, but there was no way she was going to make any snap diagnosis in front of the consultant.

'Was there a lot of blood when she was sick?' she asked.

'Not a lot, no.'

'And the colour of the blood. Was it bright red, or very dark?'

'I believe the patient said she thought she'd merely brought up some coffee until she realised it was actually blood.'

Hannah nodded. Many patients with slow-bleeding ulcers said their vomit looked exactly like coffee grounds.

'I'd do a guiac test,' she said firmly. 'If she's bleeding from a stomach ulcer—which I strongly suspect she is—

her stools will look black and tarry, and that will confirm the diagnosis.'

'You'll be pleased to know that it did,' Mr Mackay said, his smile widening. 'I've got young Kelly Ross sitting with her at the moment, but if you could pop in occasionally, to check there's no change, I'd be most grateful. She's going to have a long wait for Theatre, you see—apparently they're really busy tonight.'

Well, bully for them, Hannah thought sourly as the consultant walked away. And so much for Mr Mackay wanting her opinion. As she'd suspected, he'd simply been testing her, and at midnight on a busy Friday night she could do without someone examining her medical ability.

Slowly she began to walk down the treatment room only to discover to her surprise that Robert came after her.

'You did very well just then,' he said approvingly. 'Being grilled by a consultant in the middle of the night isn't the easiest thing in the world to handle.'

'No,' she murmured.

'And you took your time over the diagnosis, didn't say the first thing that came into your head which can always be a danger when you're put on the spot,' he continued. 'I'm really proud of you.'

'Yeah, well, thanks,' Hannah said without enthusiasm.

He shot her a puzzled glance. 'Are you OK, Hannah?'

No, she wasn't OK. She hadn't been feeling 'OK' for quite some time now, but not for the world would she ever have admitted it to anyone, far less to the special registrar.

'I'm fine, thanks.'

His gaze swept over her. 'So those dark shadows under your eyes, they're some new sort of fashion statement, are they?'

If he was trying to be smart, she didn't appreciate the joke. If he was showing true concern, she didn't think she could handle it right now.

'It's the fluorescent lighting in here,' she said tightly. 'It would make even a beauty queen look rough.'

It was true, it would, but Robert knew only too well that the fluorescent lighting couldn't possibly make her look even thinner now than when she'd first arrived two months ago. It couldn't make her face seem to consist of nothing but a pair of huge, dark eyes. And it most certainly couldn't give her a face that was paper-white and strained.

'I'd say you were anything but fine,' he declared. 'In fact, I'd say you were working too hard.'

'No harder than anybody else,' she protested.

Yes, but none of us seems to be as driven as you, he wanted to reply. None of us seems to be constantly trying to prove something, and he couldn't for the life of him think why. She was a good doctor, a dedicated one, and she had nothing to prove, least of all to him.

He tried again. 'Hannah, nobody would be surprised if you were finding working in A and E very stressful—'

'Are you saying my work isn't satisfactory?'

There it was again, he thought in confusion. The stricken look he'd seen on her face many times before. The instant assumption that he was criticising her.

'Your work is perfectly satisfactory—in fact, considerably more than satisfactory,' he replied, frowning with annoyance as he noticed Elliot coming towards them. 'All I'm saying is, if you ever feel you need help—advice—ask for it.'

'I will.' She nodded. 'If I need it.'

She wouldn't, he thought as he watched her hurry away. There was something in her that seemed to consider asking for help a sign of weakness, something that made her see an offer of help as a sign of failure, and if she wasn't careful he very much feared she was going to grind herself into the ground.

'Something wrong with Hannah?' Elliot asked curiously as he joined him.

'She's doing too much,' Robert said in exasperation. 'She looks like a ghost, and she won't accept help.'

'I seem to recall Hannah's predecessor—Dr Jarvis—being exactly the same,' Elliot observed, 'and I don't remember you offering to hold his hand. In fact, I thought you said "Good riddance" when he left.'

It was true, he had, but Robert didn't much care for the knowing, amused smile on the SHO's lips. The smile which always seemed to appear on Elliot's face whenever he voiced his worries about Hannah.

'It's not the same thing,' he retorted.

'Yeah, I can see that.' Elliot grinned, and before Robert could reply the SHO had strolled away, whistling what sounded suspiciously like 'Love is a many splendoured thing' under his breath.

Robert glared after him. So what if he was concerned about Hannah? It was his business to be concerned. She was the newest member of staff, young and inexperienced, and just because he'd never taken an interest in the welfare of a twit like Graeme Jarvis...

OK, so maybe he was having difficulty forgetting the image of a wet bathrobe clinging to a pair of small erect nipples, but that was only because he was a man, not a monk, and for Elliot to imply...

It meant nothing, he told himself angrily as he went into the office to see if the blood samples he'd taken for his patient had come back yet. All it meant was that Elliot had a weird and very warped sense of humour.

Hannah could have done with some of the SHO's sense of humour when the doors of the treatment room swung open and two paramedics pushed in a trolley carrying a young man who was bloodstained and motionless.

'There's no need to rush, Doc,' one of the paramedics

declared as she and Jane ran towards him. 'There's not a lot you can do for this one. Bullet wound to his head, and with the responses we're getting on the Glasgow coma scale I'd say he's had it.'

'Any idea what happened?' Hannah asked as the paramedics wheeled their trolley into cubicle 3, and she nevertheless began to insert an endotracheal tube, while Jane set up IV lines.

'Your guess is a good as mine,' the paramedic replied. 'Where we picked him up, people don't like to get involved. "Didn't see nothing, mate", "Didn't hear nothing, mate"—you know the kind of place.'

Hannah did. So many of their patients came from exactly the same sort of area, and at a guess she'd say it was a drug deal gone wrong. Bullet wounds were nearly always a drug deal that had gone wrong.

'Any ID?' she asked.

'Sam Armstrong, according to the letters in his pocket. We'll get Reception to check out the address but, like I said, I don't think there's any hope for him.'

Hannah didn't think there was either. The top half of Sam Armstrong's head was a crumpled mass of damaged bone and tissue. The ventilator she'd attached him to would keep him breathing, and they could monitor his blood pressure and heart rate, but that was all they could do. With his brain almost certainly irreparably damaged, he was effectively dead.

'Do you want me to page Neurology?' Jane said.

Hannah nodded. The neurosurgeon would arrange a CT scan, but from the looks of things it was merely going to be a formality.

'Nice-looking young man, too,' Jane continued. 'What a waste.'

It was an even bigger waste for the kids he'd sold drugs to, Hannah thought bitterly. She'd noticed there were no puncture marks on Sam Armstrong's arms, or in his groin. He was clearly too smart to take drugs himself. He just peddled them.

There was nothing else she could do for him, and in truth there was nothing more she wanted to do. All she wanted was to go home and go to bed, and when Elliot hurried towards her to tell her of the case of child abuse waiting in another cubicle, she most definitely wanted to go home.

'Seems the poor kid just walked into the police station, took off his shirt and showed them his back,' he declared. 'The police brought him in to us for confirmation of his injuries before they press charges. Look, I'm really sorry about this, Hannah,' he continued, seeing her expression. 'I'd take the case myself, but I've got a guy bleeding like a stuck pig in 7, Robert's working on an RTA in 2, and Mr Mackay's got what looks to be a massive stroke in 5. There's only you left to deal with it.'

'Is anybody with him? The boy, I mean?'

'I've sent Jane in to sit with him. And I'd better warn you—the kid's in a bit of a mess.'

A mess was right, Hannah thought as she went into the cubicle and found Jane cradling the child in her arms. He couldn't have been any more than eight years old and yet every part of his thin, underdeveloped little body was a mass of bruises and scars. Shiny, flat, well-healed scars which must have been inflicted when he'd been about four. Dark red ones which she guessed had been caused last year, and livid, bright red ones which had probably been inflicted as recently as yesterday.

'Why didn't he go to the police before?' Hannah said through a throat so tight it hurt.

'He said he could take it,' Jane replied huskily. 'It was when his mother started beating his little brother—'

'His *mother* did this?' Hannah gasped.

Jane nodded, her lips grim. 'Makes you think, doesn't it?'

No, it didn't make her think, Hannah decided as she catalogued every bruise, scar and lesion. It made her want to inflict similar injuries on the boy's mother, to let her see how it felt to be on the receiving end of such pain.

'What happens now?' she asked after Jane had gently helped the boy back on with his clothes.

'I should imagine he and his brother will be put into a children's home until the court case, and then they'll probably be fostered.'

'I hope they lock his mother up and throw away the key,' Hannah said grimly. 'I hope—' She stopped and frowned, suddenly aware of angry raised voices coming from outside in the treatment room. 'What on earth's going on out there?'

'I don't know,' Jane replied. 'But I've never heard Mr Mackay quite so angry.'

Neither had Hannah, and it didn't take her long to find out why.

'At last!' the A and E consultant exclaimed the minute he saw her. 'I want to know what idiot gave Mrs Forsyth a glass of water!'

'Mrs Forsyth?' she repeated in confusion.

'My slow-bleeding ulcer. Some stupid idiot gave her a glass of water, and now I'm going to have to phone Theatre to cancel surgery!'

And he would have to cancel. Even something as simple and innocuous as a glass of water could cause vomiting in an anaesthetised patient, with material from the stomach aspirated into the lungs.

'You said her husband brought her in,' Hannah observed. 'Could he have given her the water, thinking it wouldn't matter?'

'He says he didn't, and I believe him,' the consultant

replied. 'Which means it must have been one of my staff, and I want to find out who!'

She could understand his anger—she would have been furious herself—but to her dismay she suddenly noticed Kelly Ross staring at the ground as though she hoped it would open up and swallow her. Oh, no. If Mr Mackay discovered the student nurse was to blame he'd come down on her like a ton of bricks.

She took a deep breath, and steeled herself for the consultant's inevitable wrath.

'I'm afraid I can't help you, sir,' she murmured. 'I've no idea how this could have happened.'

'It's your *business* to know!' he retaliated. 'I put you in charge of this patient!'

'I realise that, sir, and I take full responsibility for what has happened,' she replied, managing to meet the consultant's blazing eyes, though her stomach was churning. 'And I can only repeat that I'm sorry, and promise it won't happen again.'

'A fat lot of use that is!' he exclaimed. 'I'm the one who's going to look as though he's in charge of a bunch of bloody fools when I phone Theatre and tell them they can't operate!' He started away angrily, then swung back, and she waited, all too aware that Jane was studiously avoiding her eye and Elliot looked deeply embarrassed. 'The neurosurgeon's just pronounced the guy in 3 clinically dead. His mother's in the relatives' waiting room. See if you can do something right for a change by asking her if she'll agree to some organ donations.'

Hannah stared after him in dismay. She hated asking relatives for organ donations. Some people reacted so badly—shouting at you, demanding to know what kind of bloodthirsty ghoul you were—and it didn't matter that Sam Armstrong was a drug dealer. His mother was still going to be devastated when she told her the situation.

'But he's still alive?' Mrs Armstrong declared when Hannah had explained how seriously injured her son was. 'You're saying he's been badly hurt, but he's still alive?'.

'Only because of the life-support machine,' Hannah said gently. 'Mrs Armstrong—'

'He's such a good boy, Doctor,' the woman interrupted. 'A lot of the kids round our way they're into drugs, stealing cars, vandalism, but Sammy...' Mrs Armstrong's small, plump face lit up with pride. 'He wants to make something of himself. I says to him, "Sammy, you work hard all day stacking shelves and sweeping floors at the supermarket. Why do you want to go to college at night? You're young, you should be out enjoying yourself." And he says, "Ma, I'm going to be somebody. I'm going to get a good job, then we can all live somewhere nice where they don't have spyholes in the doors, and bars on the windows."'

Tears welled in Hannah's eyes, and she desperately blinked them away. She didn't want to hear this. It had been easier when she'd thought Sam Armstrong was a drug-dealer, a low-life. She didn't want to know that he'd been a good son, an ambitious young man and a kind one. 'Mrs Armstrong—'

'His friend Joe—he told me what happened. He and Sammy, they were on their way home from the night college, you see, and they see this black boy attacking this white kid. Joe, he thinks they should just pass by, not get involved, but Sammy, he says, no, they gotta help. So he drags this black boy off the white kid, and the black boy— he pulls out a gun—'

'Your son was a very brave man, Mrs Armstrong, a very brave man,' Hannah interrupted, wishing the woman would just stop, wouldn't tell her any more. 'That's why my consultant was wondering whether you might be prepared to—'

'I don't have much money, Doctor,' the woman continued, pulling a battered purse out of her handbag, 'but I want you to take this to help make my Sammy well again.'

Hannah stared at the purse in dismay. 'Mrs Armstrong, it isn't a question of money—'

'I've been saving up to help Sammy with his college fees, you see. There's £200 here, Doctor. I know it's not a lot, but I clean offices at night and I can get more work, clean more offices—'

'Mrs Armstrong, there's nothing we can do!' Hannah said desperately, then bit her lip when the woman flinched. 'I'm sorry. So very sorry, but all the money in the world isn't going to make Sammy well again. There's nothing we can do. I wish there was. I truly, truly wish there was, but there isn't.'

For a long moment Mrs Armstrong stared at her, her eyes large, black pools of pain and distress, then slowly she put her purse back into her handbag. 'I see. I understand. Can I…can I see him, Doctor?'

Hannah nodded, and gently guided the woman along the corridor to the trauma room. Kelly was there, looking as grim as she herself felt, but she'd done a good job on Mrs Armstrong's son. There wasn't a mark on the young man's face. The only evidence of his horrific injury was the bandage she'd tied tightly round the top of his head.

'Would you like me to stay with you?' Hannah asked as Mrs Armstrong approached the trolley.

'No. Thank you, dear, but, no,' she replied with a tremulous smile. 'Sammy and me, we'd just like to be alone together for a little while, if you don't mind.'

Blindly Hannah went out of the trauma room. This was turning out to be a lousy shift, a really lousy shift, and it wasn't over yet. It was only four o'clock in the morning. She had another three hours to go. Another three hours before she could go home, and try to forget the grief on Mrs Armstrong's face.

And it wasn't going to be the only thing she'd have to try to forget, she realised with a sinking heart when she walked through the treatment-room doors and Mr Mackay bore down on her expectantly.

'Any luck with the organ donations, Hannah?'

She cleared her throat awkwardly. 'I'm sorry, sir, but I didn't ask. She was so upset, you see—'

'What did you expect?' the consultant exploded. 'That she'd be doing cartwheels, hanging out flags? Of all the—'

'Asking relatives to agree to organ donation is one of the toughest jobs there is, boss,' Robert said quietly as he joined them. 'You should have asked me to do it, and not expected Hannah—'

'Do you have any idea how long the waiting list is for transplants?' the consultant continued as though Robert hadn't spoken. 'Of the number of people who are waiting, hoping, for a phone call!'

'I know, sir,' Hannah began, 'and I'm sorry—'

'You're sorry. You're *sorry*?' The consultant turned a deeper shade of red. 'Where's Mrs Armstrong?'

'In the trauma room—'

'I'll speak to her myself. And as for you...' The A and E consultant didn't say she was a complete waste of space, but Hannah knew he was thinking it. 'Take a break, get yourself a cup of coffee, and get your act together!'

How was she supposed to do that? she wondered as she went slowly out of the treatment room. How could she make herself tougher, stronger, less feeble?

The truth was she couldn't. The even more unpalatable truth was that she wasn't a doctor, she would never make a doctor, and it was time she faced up to it.

Tears blurred her vision as she went into the staffroom, switched on the kettle and sat down limply on one of the old battered chairs, not realising she wasn't alone until a hand came gently down on her shoulder and she looked up to see Robert was there.

'He didn't mean it, Hannah,' he murmured, his voice soft, understanding. 'It's been a rough night, and he's simply tired like the rest of us.'

'It's not what Mr Mackay said,' she said miserably. 'Or at least, it's not just that he obviously now thinks he's hired an incompetent idiot. It's Sammy Armstrong. Robert, I took one look at him and thought, black kid, mid-twenties with a bullet wound—drug-dealer. And he wasn't—he *wasn't*!'

'Hannah—'

'What's happening to me?' she continued, knuckling her tears away, her lips trembling. 'I never used to make snap judgements about people, I never used to be so hard and uncaring. What kind of unfeeling bitch am I becoming?'

Robert pulled over another chair and sat down opposite her. 'You can't be a bitch if you care, and you wouldn't be crying if you didn't care. Hannah, you've just discovered you're human like the rest of us. You're tired, stressed—'

'I wish I was like you,' she blurted out. 'So confident, so sure of yourself.'

He shook his head ruefully. 'Would you believe there are times when I'm terrified witless?'

She stared at him in surprise. 'You're frightened?'

'Hannah, we *all* are. Frightened we'll make a mistake, frightened we'll miss something, and desperately, desperately frightened that one day we'll be so damned tired we'll kill somebody.'

'I thought it was only me who felt like that,' she murmured as he got to his feet, spooned some coffee into two cups and handed her one 'You, Elliot, Jane—you never seem to flap or panic. I thought it was just me who was scared all the time.'

'Why do you think Elliot jokes so much—or Jane and

Flo?' he asked. 'It's their way of dealing with the stress. We all have to find our own particular way of handling it.'

'What's yours?' she asked without thinking, only to colour as he smiled.

'You mean apart from generally behaving like a bear with a sore head? I switch off completely when I go home, and that's what you ought to do.'

'I suppose I could always join one of the hospital clubs—'

'Absolutely not,' he said firmly. 'You need to meet and socialise with people who aren't medical. Our world is so full of pain and heartache that you can find yourself developing a battlefield mentality if you're not careful, living for the day, seizing the moment as though it were your last. That's why so many relationships between hospital staff end in disaster. If you want to join a club, join one that doesn't have a doctor or a nurse on its books.'

Hannah gazed at him thoughtfully. Looking back, she could see she would never have become involved with Chris if she hadn't been so lonely and stressed, but Robert had sounded almost as though he was speaking from personal experience. Jane had said he'd been shattered when his wife had died, but had his marriage been in trouble before Laura's death? She would have dearly liked to have asked, but didn't dare.

'The other departments in the hospital call A and E "The Pit",' she murmured.

He nodded. 'It can seem that way at times, and it's not just because we're constantly on the receiving end of a stream of human misfortune. It's because we can never refuse to treat anyone no matter how drunk or nasty they might be.'

Hannah stared down at her cup of coffee. 'I said I wouldn't treat that horrible man who was so rude to Flo unless he agreed to let her dress his hand.'

'Did you mean it? I mean, could you really have sent him out, knowing he might bleed to death?'

She bit her lip and sighed. 'I guess not. Though I'd have made damn sure his hand hurt like hell by the time I'd finished with him,' she added belligerently.

Robert laughed, a surprisingly deep and infectious sound, but as she blew her nose and laughed too she suddenly realised how tired he looked, his black hair dishevelled, his chin showing dark stubble.

'I'm sorry to be such a wimp,' she began guiltily. 'You've got enough on your plate without—'

'It was Kelly who gave the woman with the bleeding ulcer the glass of water, wasn't it?' he interrupted.

Her heart sank and she tried to meet his gaze and couldn't. 'It might have been anyone—'

'But it was Kelly. Hannah, covering up for her was a very kind and loyal thing to do, but it was also stupid.'

'She's so very young—'

'And you're ancient, I suppose,' he said with a ghost of a smile. 'I'll have to tell Mr Mackay—'

'But—'

'Hannah, she should have known not to give any patient anything until she'd checked with a doctor, and now we're going to lose valuable—maybe vital—time before we can treat her.'

He was right, she knew he was, and she sighed. 'Just lately I seem to be getting everything wrong...'

'Will you get off that guilt trip?' he protested. 'You're a good doctor.'

'Not a gifted or a talented one,' she said a little wistfully, and to her surprise his grey eyes suddenly became cold.

'Is that what you want?' Robert demanded. 'You can't be happy simply being a good doctor—you've got to be some high-flying, brilliant one instead?'

In truth, she wanted only to be as good as she could be,

but she didn't want him to think she was lacking in initiative, a non-achiever, or worse.

'Would it be so very wrong if I were ambitious?' she said, taking a sip of her coffee to buy herself some time.

He hadn't used to think it was, Robert remembered. In fact, he'd applauded Laura's ambition until they'd got married and he'd discovered just how very ambitious she'd been. If Hannah felt the same—that promotion was more important than anything else—then he had all the more reason to keep his distance, to clamp down hard on his body's unsettling reaction to her.

'It depends on why you decided to become a doctor,' he replied, his eyes fixed on her. 'If your aim is to find some new treatment then I'll support you all the way, but if you see the profession as a means of gaining power and status, a giant ego trip...'

Hannah had never wanted to be as successful as her father, not ever. All she'd ever wanted had been to help people, to make them well again, but would he think her naïve, and childish, if she said that?

'I suppose so,' she muttered, and to her surprise he abruptly got to his feet.

'Ambition can be a two-edged sword, Hannah,' he said tightly. 'Handle it with care.'

His face was all dark planes and shadows under the harsh fluorescent lighting, and she didn't know what to say. All she knew was that somehow she'd said the wrong thing, and she desperately wanted to make it right.

'Robert—'

'Sorry to interrupt, Robert,' Jane said, popping her head breathlessly round the staffroom door, 'but it's bedlam out here, and if Mr Mackay doesn't get help soon I think he's going to burst a blood vessel.'

'I'm coming,' he replied, but as Hannah got to her feet

he shook his head firmly. 'Take another ten minutes, finish your coffee.'

'I've had enough—'

'Sit down and drink your coffee, Hannah,' he ordered, and as Jane disappeared again Hannah's lips twitched.

'What was that you were saying about ego trips, and some doctors loving the power?'

A smile of genuine amusement lit up his face. 'You're feeling better, I see.'

'I am, thanks to you,' she replied, then grimaced. 'I always seem to be thanking you, don't I?'

'You'll be all right, Hannah,' he declared. 'You have great compassion and dedication. Hold onto those two things, and you'll be fine.'

She nodded, but he must have seen a trace of lingering doubt in her face because he suddenly reached out and tilted her chin upwards with his fingers.

'No more self-flagellation, OK? No more agonising.'

She laughed a little shakily. 'I'll try my best.'

'You do that.' He smiled, but as he continued to gaze down at her his smile slowly disappeared, to be replaced by a look that made her heart begin to race, her breath catch in her throat.

'Hannah…'

She could hear the banging doors, the hum of conversation and clatter of trolley wheels on vinyl in the corridor outside, but all she was really aware of was that something was happening that she didn't understand.

'Robert…'

He took a step forward and she forgot to breathe as he cupped her face with his hands. He was going to kiss her again—she knew he was—and he did, but not as she had expected.

He simply tilted her head and placed a kiss on her forehead. A kiss that was as gentle and tender as it was frustratingly brief.

'You're a nice kid, Hannah, a great kid,' he murmured, his voice suddenly rough, husky. 'Try not to change.'

And with that he walked away, leaving her staring blankly after him. A nice kid? He thought she was a great *kid*?

He hadn't thought she was a child that night in his flat. He hadn't thought she was a child when he'd kissed her, and held her. And she didn't want him to think of her as a child. She wanted...

Oh, she was so damned confused she didn't know what she wanted any more, but it was certainly not for Robert to think of her as a kid!

CHAPTER SIX

'SO, YOU'RE quite happy with Hannah's work, then?' Mr Mackay asked, shuffling the papers on his desk and determinedly avoiding his special registrar's eye.

'More than happy,' Robert replied with surprise. 'Boss, if you're still concerned about that fiasco with the bleeding stomach ulcer case, and Sam Armstrong—'

'Kelly has been reprimanded for her part in the affair, and as Mrs Armstrong agreed to donate some of her son's organs after I'd spoken to her I consider the subject closed. I simply wondered...' The consultant shuffled his papers again. 'As Hannah's been with us now for two months, I merely wondered how you felt she was settling in, whether there were any problems.'

A slight frown creased Robert's forehead. 'Did you expect there to be any?'

'Good grief, no!' Mr Mackay exclaimed with what he hoped was a suitably reassuring smile, though in reality he was already beginning to wish he'd never started this conversation.

He wouldn't have either if Charles Blake hadn't rung him up yesterday completely out of the blue, clearly worried about his daughter.

Initially he hadn't blamed the man. Hell, he had two grown-up daughters himself and the last branch of medicine he'd have wanted either of them to specialise in was A and E, but what had worried him—more than worried him— was Charles Blake's apparent fear that Hannah might not be pulling her weight. It had been an odd thing for a father to say—a very odd thing—and the more the A and E consultant had thought about it, the more uneasy he'd become.

'So you have no worries about her work?' he pressed.

'None at all,' Robert declared. 'She's a good doctor, and she'll become an excellent one in time. She suffers from a severely over-developed inferiority complex, but apart from that I can find no fault with her.'

The consultant nodded. He suspected he'd have a huge inferiority complex too, if his father had undermined his confidence the way Charles Blake clearly did his daughter's. The man might have a string of qualifications and awards to his name, but he clearly merited a big fat zero on the sensitivity scale.

'Boss, this sudden concern of yours with Hannah,' Robert continued, his frown deepening. 'Is there something I should know—something you're not telling me?'

The consultant's heart sank. He'd promised Hannah he wouldn't tell anyone who her father was, appreciating her desire to be accepted for herself, but he'd also had his own reasons for wanting to keep her parentage a secret.

Robert Cunningham would blow a fuse when he found out. Born into a poor, working-class family, Robert had no time for rich, well-connected students, and the minute he found out who Hannah's father was he'd undoubtedly accuse her of pulling strings to get the job. It wouldn't make a blind bit of difference to point out that nobody in their right mind would pull strings to get a job at St Stephen's.

'Of course there's nothing you should know,' the consultant protested. 'Look, I don't have to explain my interest to you,' he continued, taking refuge in anger. 'This is my department and it's part of my job to keep my finger on the pulse!'

'Yes, but—'

'I have to go,' the consultant said abruptly, getting to his feet fast. 'I've a meeting with Admin in ten minutes, and you...I suggest you get back to work!'

And before Robert could reply his boss had made a bee-line for the door and was gone, leaving him gazing blankly after him.

What in the world had that been all about? Robert wondered as he left the consultant's office and walked down the corridor. Normally Mr Mackay was only too pleased to leave the supervision of the junior members of staff to him, and yet the consultant had looked almost guilty when he'd asked him if there was anything he should know.

In fact, if the consultant had been a younger man he'd even have started to wonder if his interest in Hannah was more than strictly professional, but his boss was a happily married man of some twenty-five years, and he...

Was becoming fixated, Robert decided as he pushed open the doors of the treatment room and felt his pulse rate rocket when he saw Hannah laughing at something Jane had just said.

Dammit, she was just a girl. A girl who possessed a pair of beautiful dark eyes and wonderfully curly hair, but she was still just a girl. He might well be attracted to her—OK, all right, he admitted it—but that didn't mean he had to give in to that attraction. He was a mature adult male, not a teenager, and it was about time he started acting like one.

The only trouble was that it was a hell of a lot easier to think about than actually do, he realised with a groan as Hannah suddenly threw back her head and laughed again and he felt his groin tighten painfully. A hell of a lot easier.

'RTA on the way, Robert!' Floella suddenly called. 'Teenage couple—the bloke sounds to be in much worse shape than the girl.'

Which was exactly what he needed, Robert told himself as he strode towards the trauma room. Work. To bury himself in work, and maybe that would also bury his intrusive and relentless libido.

And it did. At least it did until he and Elliot had stabilised the young man and sent him to Intensive Care, and he went in search of Hannah to see how she was coping with the injured female passenger.

'She's conscious, knows who and where she is, and she can move her arms and legs,' Hannah reported. 'The only thing she's complaining about is some pain in her neck.'

Robert nodded, and noticed with approval that not only had Hannah kept on the cervical collar which had been placed around the girl's neck at the scene of the accident, she'd also immobilised her on a hard board.

'Have you paged Radiology yet?' he asked.

'Jerry Clark's on his way down now.'

Oh, he was, was he? Robert thought grimly.

Ever since Hannah had told him about the X-ray technician's behaviour he'd had to keep his temper under a very tight rein whenever Jerry Clark appeared. And the rein got even tighter today when Jerry breezed into the cubicle with a smile at Hannah that made Robert's fingers itch to rearrange the technician's plump features.

'Neck and back X-rays only, please, Jerry,' he said brusquely, before turning his attention back to the young girl lying nervously on the trolley. 'Dr Blake tells me your neck's very sore. Do you feel any numbness or tingling in your hands and feet?'

'None at all,' she replied. 'How's my boyfriend? Nobody will tell me anything—'

'You just lie there and relax, and let us do the worrying,' Robert interrupted smoothly. 'Aren't those X-rays ready yet, Jerry?' he continued, frowning across at the technician.

'They are, and they're negative. No sign of any damage to the neck and back at all.'

Hannah breathed a sigh of relief. A broken neck and

subsequent paralysis was always a possibility after a bad road accident like this, but luckily the girl was fine.

'I suggest you give her a complete check-over in case she's sustained fractures anywhere else,' Robert commented. 'The cervical collar can come off now—'

'Sorry, Robert, but could you come right away?' Floella said anxiously, popping her head through the cubicle curtains. 'We've got a guy in 7 who looks to be haemorrhaging pretty badly.'

He was already walking towards the staff nurse and Hannah smiled encouragingly at the girl. 'You heard what the man said. Have you any other aches and pains I should know about?'

'My knee and arm hurt a bit,' the girl admitted.

'Jerry, can I have X-rays of the right knee and arm?'

'Your wish is my command, sweetheart,' he replied with what Hannah presumed he considered his most ingratiating smile, and she turned her back on him irritably.

How Jerry had ever got it into his head that he was irresistible to women was beyond her. Elliot was irresistible to women, and Robert...

No, she wasn't going to think about Robert, she told herself firmly. She'd been doing her level best for the past few days not to think about Robert, and she was actually succeeding. Well, some of the time she was. Occasionally she was. Now and then she was.

'Definite fractured right knee and arm,' Jerry declared. 'I'd better get going. Unless, of course, there's something else you'd like me to do for you?'

How about going and playing on the motorway in the rush hour? Hannah thought sourly as he leered across at her on his way out, but when the girl lying on the trolley uttered a small moan, she forgot all about the technician.

'What's wrong?' she asked, going quickly over to her.

'It's my neck. It's really, really sore. Do you think I could have a pillow?'

There had been no sign of any back or neck injuries on the X-rays. The girl wasn't complaining of any numbness or tingling in her arms and legs, so there was no earthly reason why she shouldn't have a pillow, and yet suddenly Hannah felt uneasy.

'Try this and see if this helps,' she suggested, folding the smallest towel she could find and slipping it under the girl's head.

You're wasting time, her mind whispered as she hovered beside the trolley. The waiting room's packed and as the girl's been thoroughly X-rayed there's no need for her to still be in the treatment room. You should be sending her along to the plastering department to have her knee and arm set. But something, a small nagging little doubt at the back of her mind, just wouldn't go away.

'Does it feel any better with the towel under your head?' she asked.

'Sort of.' The girl frowned. 'My neck doesn't hurt nearly so much but my fingers have gone all tingly.'

'Have they?' Hannah said with a calmness she was very far from feeling. Gently she slid the towel out from under the young girl's head, though all her instincts were urging her to yank it away fast. 'I won't be a minute,' she continued, walking towards the cubicle curtains. 'There's just...just something I want to check on.'

'Fine.' The girl smiled, but Hannah knew she was anything but 'fine', and the second she was out of the cubicle she began to run.

'Right, page the neurosurgeon and get Jerry Clark back immediately,' Robert ordered when Hannah explained what had happened. 'You're sure the only time you moved her was to slide the towel under her head, and then to take it away again?'

Hannah nodded.

'OK, put the cervical collar back on, and when Jerry shows up I want to be there.'

And he was, with a vengeance.

'I want more X-rays, Jerry, and this time I want them done properly,' he said curtly.

'Properly?' the technician repeated, his face going from white to red in quick succession. 'Are you calling my professional competence into question?'

Robert would have dearly liked to have accused him of a lot more, but right now he didn't have the time, not with the neurological surgeon on his way down to give a second opinion.

'Jerry, I want more X-rays,' he said again, his voice ice-cold. 'Either you take them for us or I can ask your boss to come down and do the honours. The choice is yours.'

Jerry took them.

'Well, would you look at that?' the neurosurgeon muttered when he joined them and studied the new set of X-ray plates. 'I'm not surprised it wasn't noticed before. It's so faint even I can hardly see it, and if Hannah hadn't mentioned the tingling in her fingers I would never have thought to look for it.'

The young girl had broken her second cervical vertebrae. Nerves to her entire body passed through this bone, nerves that controlled her breathing, movement, and feeling.

'How do your fingers feel now?' Robert asked, turning to the girl on the trolley.

'They're not tingling any more,' she replied, 'but my neck's sore again.'

Hannah met Robert's eyes with relief. The girl might have broken her neck and would have to wear a brace screwed into her head for the next few months, but if they hadn't got that second set of X-rays, if she'd been moved without the support of a cervical collar, she would have been paralysed for life.

'Well done,' Robert said to Hannah after the neurosurgeon had transferred the girl up to his ward. 'What made you suspect something was wrong?'

'I don't know,' she admitted. 'Call it a gut feeling—intuition, perhaps.'

'Then I suggest you immediately start cultivating both,' he said warmly. 'That sort of talent could be worth its weight in gold in A and E.'

She smiled, but when he did, too, a slight sigh escaped her.

He had such a nice smile when he cared to use it. Such a very nice smile. The trouble was that it would keep inducing that unsettling fluttering sensation deep in the pit of her stomach. It would persist in resurrecting the silly thoughts and feelings she kept having about him—thoughts and feelings which she knew perfectly well *were* silly until he smiled at her.

'I must go,' she mumbled. 'We're mobbed as usual—'

'You're looking a little better,' he interrupted. 'Have you been taking my advice—getting out more?'

'Sort of,' she replied. 'I've started going for long walks when I finish work. I used to walk a lot at home in Edinburgh—I found it cleared my head, helped me to sleep better—and it seems to be helping.'

'You walk on your own at night?' Robert said, aghast.

Just the thought of what could happen to her, doing that, was enough to make his blood run cold. Then offer to walk with her, the little voice in his mind said, and he all but laughed out loud at the suggestion. Dammit, he knew he'd like nothing better than to walk with her, to make sure she was safe, but if he couldn't control his intrusive libido in a crowded place like St Stephen's, God knew what would happen if he walked alone with her at night.

But he knew one thing for sure. He had to put an end to her nightly strolls.

'Hannah, walking alone in London at night—it's not a good idea.'

'You're not going to give me the "London isn't Edinburgh" speech again, are you?' she groaned. 'Look, I'm not an idiot. I don't walk in the parks, or down lonely streets. I stick to places where there are lots of people.'

'I don't give a damn if you walk in Piccadilly Circus!' he burst out. 'Promise me you'll stop doing it!'

'Oh, for heaven's sake…'

'Promise me, Hannah,' he insisted. 'And no crossing your fingers behind your back when you're doing it,' he added, correctly reading her mind.

A splutter of laughter came from her. 'I didn't know you were a mind-reader.'

'There's a lot of things you don't know about me,' he said, grinning.

He *grinned*? Robert Cunningham could grin like a regular, normal person?

He was right, there was a lot she didn't know about him. But you'd like to find out, wouldn't you? her mind said, and she determinedly trampled on the little voice.

'OK, I promise,' she said. 'But I still think you're being silly.'

He thought he was, too, as she walked away, but not in the way Hannah meant.

Why did he like her so much? And it was liking now, as well as lust. He liked her freshness, her total lack of guile. He admired her honesty, even if he often thought she was far too hard on herself.

In fact, if he was going to be really honest, he liked everything about her. The way she looked, the way she smiled. Her courage and dedication. Hell, he even liked the way she caught her lower lip between her teeth when she was puzzling something out. The way she blew the curls away from her face with an impatient huff when she was angry.

But it was a liking that could go nowhere. Even if she liked him—and he thought she did—there could be no future for them.

He couldn't give her what she needed. He didn't think he could give any girl that any more. Laura had managed not only to destroy his love during their marriage but also his ability to trust, and without trust there was nothing.

It was better to keep his distance from Hannah Blake, he decided as he saw her deep in conversation with a member of the local fire brigade, a slight frown on her face. Better for her, for him, for everybody.

'What's the problem?' he asked, his professional instincts instantly clicking into place as Hannah walked quickly towards him.

'What do you know about taps?' she asked, her lips twitching slightly.

'Taps?' He frowned.

'Bath taps. The fire brigade have just brought in a Mr and Mrs Fuller. The couple got married this afternoon and are booked into a hotel honeymoon suite for the weekend. Apparently Mrs Fuller decided to have a bath as they'd had such a long drive down from Shrewsbury, but the water felt a little hot after she got in, and when she was trying to turn on the cold water tap with her toes—'

'She's a contortionist, is she?'

'Of course not.' Hannah laughed. 'You don't have to be a contortionist to turn off taps with your toes. I do it all the time.'

'You do?' he said faintly.

'It's quite easy really, and Mrs Fuller would probably have been fine if she hadn't added so much bubble bath to the water and made the bath slippery.' Hannah frowned.

'Actually, it's something I'd better remember myself. I tend to be a bit heavy-handed, too, when it comes to bubble bath.'

Robert wished she hadn't said that. He *really* wished she hadn't said that. He was already having a hard enough time trying to crush down the image which had sprung into his mind of Hannah naked in a bath. Hannah pink and glowing. Hannah with little droplets of water running down between—

And now she'd gone and added bubbles to his mental picture. White, frothy bubbles that probably clung, and slid, and—

'I presume the fire brigade have cut off the tap at its base?' he said quickly.

She nodded. 'They're suggesting we try using something called a whizzer saw. Apparently it has a diamond tip and they use it for cutting through steel rings, but its main drawback is we'd have to turn off any oxygen in the vicinity.'

'I know,' Robert replied. 'I've used one before.'

'You have?' Hannah said in amazement. 'I didn't realise so many people got their big toes stuck up taps.'

'They don't. The particular case I worked on wasn't a tap, and it wasn't attached to the patient's toe, but it did require a whizzer saw to remove it.'

Something about the pinkness of his cheeks made Hannah decide she'd rather not know what he'd removed, and from where, and instead she said, 'Would you come and take a look at Mrs Fuller, and see what we can do?'

Judging by Mrs Fuller's mortified expression as he strode through the cubicle curtains, Robert thought the new bride would have been quite happy if he'd suggested amputating her toe.

'I have never been so embarrassed in all my life,' she wailed while her husband patted her hand soothingly. 'The indignity of it. Carried out of the honeymoon suite and down through the hotel lobby on a stretcher by the fire brigade—'

'It would have been all right if you hadn't sat up and told everyone you weren't ill,' her husband pointed out. 'People would have been sympathetic.'

'And they would have thought I'd had a stroke or a heart attack,' she protested. 'I couldn't let them think that. It would have been a wicked thing to do.'

'So we got all the comments instead,' he said with sigh. '"Cor!" and "That must have been some wedding night!" being the only ones I'd care to repeat in mixed company.'

Hannah bit down hard on her lip, and said a little unsteadily, 'Would it be worth applying some ice, do you think?'

Robert shook his head. 'It's the toe inside the tap that's swollen, and applying ice to the rest of the foot isn't going to help. I'm afraid it's going to have to be the whizzer saw.'

It sounded terrifying. It looked even worse when Robert switched it on. And when he brought it down on the tap and a great plume of sparks shot up into the air, Hannah could see why the fire brigade had insisted that all oxygen in the vicinity had to be switched off.

Being blown to bits clearly wasn't of the utmost concern to Mrs Fuller. She let out a scream that all but shattered Hannah's eardrums, sat bolt upright on the trolley and shrieked, 'Switch it off! I've changed my mind! I'll live with the tap—buy bigger shoes, go barefoot!'

'It's going to be all right, Mrs Fuller,' Hannah declared, holding her firmly. 'Dr Cunningham knows what he's doing.' At least she hoped he did. 'It will only take a few minutes…'

It did, but it seemed like an eternity before Robert straightened up with a pleased smile.

'One tap—slightly the worse for wear, I'm afraid—removed as promised,' he announced, holding it out to Mrs Fuller.

Mrs Fuller looked as though she didn't know whether to laugh or cry, and opted for blowing her nose instead. 'I'm so sorry, Doctor. Screaming, and bawling, and carrying on like that—'

'There's absolutely no need to apologise,' Robert interrupted. 'I doubt if anyone would have sat quietly while somebody took a saw to their foot. How does the toe feel?'

'Sore,' she admitted.

'Can you move it at all?' he asked.

She could, and luckily it didn't appear as though she had suffered any lasting damage. Her foot would be pretty painful for a few days if she tried to put any weight on it, but apart from that she'd survived unscathed from her ordeal with the tap.

'I bet she never tries to turn off a tap with her toes again,' Jane said when Mr and Mrs Fuller had gone, taking the remnants of the bath tap with them as a souvenir. 'Can't you just imagine the kind of ribbing they're going to get for the rest of their honeymoon?'

'The fire chief told me the hotel is actually going to charge them for damage to the honeymoon suite,' Hannah said in disbelief. 'OK, so maybe she's wrecked the bath, but most honeymooners don't spend their wedding night in the bath, do they?'

Robert didn't suppose they did, but it certainly opened up a whole array of interesting thoughts. Thoughts he'd far rather not have, he decided as he felt a tide of dark colour creeping up the back of his neck.

'Something I can do for you, Kelly?' he asked, noticing the student nurse hovering nearby, clearly trying to attract his attention.

'It's the patient in cubicle 7, Dr Cunningham,' she began as Jane walked away, still laughing about Mrs Fuller's predicament. 'Dr Mathieson says he's just suffering from minor cuts and bruises—the man was mugged, you see—but...'

'But?' Robert pressed, confused as Kelly's voice trailed away into silence.

'The thing is...' The student nurse gazed unhappily up at him. 'The thing is, he's got Aids, Dr Cunningham, and Dr Mathieson has asked me to clean his cuts, and—'

'And if you put on a pair of latex gloves while you're treating him, the chances of you catching it are nil unless you feel there's a danger you might suddenly be seized by an overwhelming desire to make love to him!' Robert said tartly.

Scarlet colour swept over Kelly's face and bright tears shimmered in her eyes. 'I know that, Doctor, but, you see, my brother—he died last year of Aids. It's one of the reasons I decided to become a nurse, and the patient—Mr Seller—seeing him, it reminds me—'

'Why didn't you say so in the first place?' Robert asked quickly, compassion and sympathy plain on his face. 'I'll look after him for you—'

'I'll do it, Robert,' Hannah broke in. 'You're just going off duty.'

'So are you,' he pointed out, glancing up at the treatment-room clock.

'Yes, but it will only take me half an hour—'

'Fifteen minutes if we share,' he interrupted. 'And I bet I've got more experience of Aids patients than you do,' he added as a clincher.

No amount of experience was going to help Colin Seller, Hannah thought as she gazed sadly down at the young man's ravaged body. In fact, she doubted if anything could. He had all the classic outward symptoms of advanced Aids, and it wasn't a pretty sight. Small, fluid-filled blisters—herpes simplex—covered his face, and Kaposi's sarcoma—

tumours consisting of blue-red nodules—had already begun to appear on his feet, legs and arms.

'I understand you've been mugged, Mr Seller?' she said, gently beginning to clean the cuts on his face and arms.

He nodded. 'Crazy, isn't it? You'd think it would have been obvious to anyone that I don't have any money.'

It should have been. Colin Seller's clothes might be clean and neat but they were obviously old and his shoes had holes in them.

'Your Aids,' she continued as Robert began removing the dirt from the cuts in Colin Seller's legs. 'What sort of medication are you taking to keep it under control?'

The man shrugged. 'No point in controlling it. It's going to kill me eventually so why postpone the inevitable?'

'But if you don't take any medication—'

'The tumours will affect my gastrointestinal and respiratory tracts, causing severe internal bleeding, and lymphoma of the brain. And if I'm real lucky I might get toxoplasmosis which can lead to lung and heart damage and severe encephalitis.' Colin Seller smiled as Hannah stared at him, open-mouthed. 'I've got Aids, Doctor. That doesn't mean I'm brainless. At least not yet.'

'Then why don't you take the drugs we can give you?' she protested. 'OK, so they may not be able to cure you, but at least we might be able to keep you alive until we can find a cure.'

'Doctor, I've lost my lover to Aids, my family have disowned me, and I've no job, no home, no nothing. Sometimes…sometimes living just gets too painful, and you'd prefer not do it any more.'

She put down the piece of gauze she'd been using and clasped the young man's hand in her own. 'I'm sorry. I know that's a really dumb and inadequate thing to say, but I'm truly, truly sorry.'

Colin Seller clearly didn't think it was dumb, and neither did Robert as he stared across at her.

She meant it, he realised. She wasn't just mouthing the stock set of comforting phrases they all learnt at med school. Hannah truly meant it.

Laura hadn't possessed one tenth of the compassion of this girl. She might have been the most brilliant junior doctor he'd ever met, but personal success had meant everything to her, and the emotional needs of her patients had come a very poor second.

And not just her patients' emotional needs, he remembered with a twist of pain. The night she'd died he'd accused her of wanting the acclaim and fame that medicine could bring more than she wanted him, and she'd told him that even if he was content to work for the rest of his life in a run-down dump like St Stephen's, she wasn't. And it had been then that he'd told her he wanted a divorce. Then that he'd known their marriage was over, and that it should never have occurred in the first place.

'I think it's time you went home, Hannah,' he said with an effort, hearing the babble of voices outside that heralded the arrival of the night staff. 'It will only take me a couple of minutes to finish up in here.'

'But—'

'Home, Hannah,' he insisted, leading her purposefully towards the cubicle curtains. 'It's late, and you've done enough.'

'But—'

'You do what the man says, Doctor.' Colin Seller grinned, his cruelly disfigured face lighting up with amusement. 'Seems to me like you need someone to take care of you.'

It seemed that way to Robert, too, but he couldn't be that man, and he knew he couldn't.

'I just wish there was something more we could do for

him,' Hannah sighed as Robert propelled her through the curtains.

'I think you already have,' he murmured.

'I know it's his choice not to take any medication,' she continued as though Robert hadn't spoken, 'but if there was only something else we could do. Something that would make him a little more comfortable.'

'Perhaps there is. Now, off you go,' he concluded, giving her a gentle nudge. 'And no more taking long walks on your own, remember?'

'Aye-aye, sir,' she replied, standing smartly to attention, and chuckled as she heard the clear sound of his laughter following her out of the treatment room.

It had been an odd day, she decided as she collected her coat and bag from the staffroom. That young girl earlier in the afternoon who could so easily have been paralysed, the honeymoon couple...

Her lips curved as she walked out through the waiting room. The poor girl had been so mortified, and her husband had been terrific. It must be wonderful to have someone care that much for you. To have someone love you so much that only your welfare mattered.

Colin Seller didn't have anyone who cared for him, she thought sadly as she walked out of the hospital, shivering slightly at the contrast in temperatures. She so wished they could have done something for him, something to help him, but she couldn't think what.

You're a doctor, Hannah, not a social worker, she told herself firmly as she turned up her coat collar against the falling sleet. You can only do what you can do. But as she paused at the kerb she suddenly noticed that Robert was crossing the street ahead of her, and a slight frown creased her forehead.

He was walking oddly, skirting the icy puddles, carefully avoiding the potholes in the road, and as she continued to watch him she suddenly saw why. He wasn't wearing any shoes.

He'd given them to Colin Seller. She knew without a shadow of a doubt that he'd given them to the young man, and a hard lump formed in her throat as she stared after him, watching his painful progress, his head bent low against the biting wind. There *had* been something they could do for Colin Seller, and Robert had done it. Not given him a long lecture on the importance of taking his drugs, or a reprimand for failing to do so, but given him something which showed that somebody cared about his welfare.

And it was in that split second that she suddenly realised something else. Something she should have known before—perhaps *had* known before—and hadn't wanted to admit.

She'd fallen in love with Robert Cunningham. Somehow, some way, she'd managed to fall in love with this difficult, prickly, oh, so nice man, but the trouble was, she didn't know what she was going to do about it.

CHAPTER SEVEN

'MR MAITLAND was brought in by his wife about ten minutes ago,' Robert explained as Hannah accompanied him down the treatment room. 'He has a high fever, stiff neck and also seems to be slightly confused and disorientated. His wife is terrified he has meningitis.'

Hannah nodded. Even the word was enough to strike terror into most people's hearts, but it didn't need to. If the condition was diagnosed early, the prognosis for a full recovery was usually excellent.

'Nobody is really certain what causes meningitis, are they?' she observed. 'All we know for certain is that an infection must have entered the cerebrospinal fluid which surrounds and protects the brain and spinal cord.'

'That's right.'

'And you're going to do a spinal tap to see if Mr Maitland's cerebrospinal fluid is infected?'

Robert smiled as he led the way into cubicle 5. 'No, I'm not. You are.'

She stumbled in dismay as she followed him. She'd thought he was going to show her how the procedure was done, not that she was going to do it herself. She was sure that's what he'd said. 'Robert, I really don't think—'

'Any change in Mr Maitland's condition, Flo?' he asked, completely ignoring Hannah's panic-stricken appeal.

'No deterioration that I can see,' the staff nurse replied.

'Good, good.' He nodded. 'OK, Hannah, we've anaesthetised the skin overlying the lumbar vertebrae so what I want you to do first is to press your thumb into the middle

115

of Mr Maitland's back, then gradually move your thumb down the bony prominences.'

Robert quite clearly wasn't going to take no for an answer—not when he was already holding the box of latex gloves out to her—and reluctantly she took a pair, and even more reluctantly pulled them on.

'What am I looking for when I'm moving my thumb down Mr Maitland's back?' she asked.

'The undulations of the spinal column as you get nearer to his buttocks.'

'The undulations?' Hannah repeated.

'Each one is a single vertebra, and we're looking for the third and fourth, which are just above the base of the spine. Look, let me help you,' he continued, moving behind her and placing his hand over hers as she gazed uncertainly up at him. 'The secret is not to be too tentative. You can't possibly hurt bone simply by pressing it.'

She knew that, but she also knew it would have been considerably easier for her to concentrate if it hadn't been Robert showing her the technique. If it hadn't been his hand guiding hers, and his subtle aftershave she could smell, and his chest resting against her back.

How had she fallen in love with this man? Why had she fallen in love with him? She didn't know him—not really—but she knew with absolute certainty that it wasn't simply a physical attraction she felt for him any more. She cared about him. She worried about him. And she wanted to see him smiling and happy, instead of sad and strained all the time.

'I—I can feel the vertebrae,' she stammered, deliberately not looking up at him. 'What do I do now?'

A hollow, very fine needle appeared before her eyes.

'Insert this between the third and fourth vertebrae to pierce the meninges that covers the spinal cord, and extract some fluid for analysis.'

This time she did look up at him, but in total panic. What if she put the needle in the wrong place? What if she paralysed Mr Maitland?

'You can't do any damage, Hannah,' Robert continued gently, correctly interpreting her expression. 'The spinal cord only goes as far as the lower portion of the middle of the back, and as you'll be inserting the needle into an area well below that, you can't possibly do Mr Maitland any harm.'

That was easy for him to say, she thought as she gingerly inserted the needle. He'd probably done hundreds—OK, maybe nearer dozens—of spinal taps. This was her first.

'I've got it!' she said in amazement as the cerebrospinal fluid shot up into the needle without any effort at all. 'I've actually done it!'

'I said it was easy, didn't I?' he replied, but as she turned and beamed up at him, his heart twisted inside him.

It was his own fault, of course. Offering to help her, using that as a feeble excuse to stand close to her, to hold her lightly, if only for a few seconds. It was the kind of sick ploy someone like Jerry Clark would have used, and if he now felt like hell it was his own just deserts.

Not if you're falling in love with her, his mind whispered, and unconsciously he shook his head.

He wasn't falling in love with her. OK, so he liked her. OK, so he seemed to spend an inordinate amount of his time thinking about her, but that was just physical attraction. Love was for teenagers. Love was just desire and sex wrapped up in a romantic name. He'd been down that road once, and he didn't want to go down it again—ever.

'So, what do we do now?' Hannah asked.

God alone knows, Robert thought, only to realise from her expectant expression that she was referring to something entirely different.

'Flo will send the sample off to the lab,' he said quickly.

'They'll check it out for bacteria and white blood cells, then get back to us.'

'I presume if it *is* meningitis, it's going to be meningo-coccal?' Hannah remarked as she followed him out of the cubicle. 'At thirty-eight, Mr Maitland's not likely to have contracted pneumococcal meningitis, although I under-stand—'

She didn't get the chance to say what she understood because the doors of the treatment room suddenly slammed open and a young man appeared, wide-eyed, sweating and dishevelled.

'Can somebody help me, please?' he yelled. 'My wife—she's out in the van, and she's in labour!'

Hannah was halfway through the waiting room, clutching the obs kit, before she realised Robert was with her.

'I thought maybe two heads might be better than one,' he said with a grin. 'I mean, childbirth isn't exactly our speciality, is it?'

It wasn't, and when Hannah clambered into the back of the van and saw the young man's wife, her legs wide apart and the top of a little dark head protruding from her vagina, she was more than relieved to have Robert with her.

'Just as well I told Jane to page the labour ward,' Robert observed, pulling off his sweater and rolling up his sleeves. 'It looks as though mum's cut it a bit fine.'

A bit fine was right. With a sharp cry the woman sud-denly bore down heavily, and Robert only just got his hands up in time to catch the tiny scrap of humanity as it shot out of its mother.

'My baby?' the woman gasped, trying to lever herself upright. 'Is my baby all right?'

'She's fine,' Robert replied, wrapping the baby in his sweater after Hannah had clamped and cut the cord. 'You have a beautiful baby daughter.'

And she *was* beautiful, Hannah thought, staring down

into a pair of enormous blue eyes. Wet and bloody, but bright-eyed and alert, and quite, quite beautiful.

'I think you've got a fan there,' she commented, seeing the baby snuggle into Robert's chest as members of the labour ward arrived and whisked the mother away to the delivery room to deliver the placenta.

He shook his head wryly. 'I'm afraid she's labouring under a grave misapprehension. My sole contribution to her arrival in the world was to catch her as she shot past.'

'Yes, but, boy, what a catch.' Hannah laughed, then glanced around with a slight frown. 'What happened to the father?'

'He keeled over the moment you dashed out of the treatment room. Kelly's probably reviving him with tea and sympathy even as we speak.'

She chuckled. 'Poor man. I bet he'll never forget his daughter's arrival.' She tickled the little girl under her chin. 'She is lovely, isn't she?'

'Yes. Yes, she is.'

Robert's voice was soft, husky, but when she glanced up at him he wasn't looking at the baby at all, but at her.

Did he mean he found her attractive, desirable? Did he mean what she hoped—oh, how she hoped—he meant? Her breath seemed to be wedged somewhere in the centre of her chest but she managed an uncertain smile. 'They say... People say...all babies are beautiful.'

'Do they?' he murmured, his eyes catching and holding hers. 'Then I guess...if everyone says that...'

She couldn't have looked away if she'd tried She couldn't have moved if she'd wanted to. Something in his eyes—something that sent a quiver of sensation running through her body—held her rooted to the spot, and when he cleared his throat huskily, she held her breath expectantly.

'Hannah—'

'Dr Cunningham, this is *most* unprofessional!' Sister Strachan from the special care baby unit declared, appearing in front of them without warning. 'It's well below freezing out here and this…' She fingered Robert's sweater with clear distaste. 'This is hardly adequate clothing for a newborn.'

'You're perfectly right,' he replied as she held out her arms and reluctantly he handed the baby to her. 'I'm sorry, Sister.'

'Name?'

He gazed at her in confusion. 'Dr Robert Cunningham. Special registrar, A and E—'

'The *baby's* name, Doctor,' Sister Strachan interrupted in exasperation. 'All kinds of complications can arise in SCBU if we don't know this little mite's surname.'

Robert looked even more shamefaced. 'I don't think we actually got the baby's surname, did we, Dr Blake?'

Sister Strachan's eyes rolled heavenwards when Hannah shook her head, and with a look that spoke volumes she clutched the baby to her ample bosom and strode away, muttering darkly.

'Bang goes my credibility in SCBU for the foreseeable future,' Robert sighed as he led the way back into A and E.

'Maybe she might forgive us if we send up little Miss No Name's father once he's recovered from the shock?' Hannah suggested.

He shook his head and laughed. 'Not a hope, I'm afraid. We're dead ducks as far as Sister Strachan is concerned.'

Hannah laughed, too, but as she followed him back into the treatment room her main emotion was frustration. Somehow she sensed that he'd been about to say something momentous just before Sister Strachan had interrupted him, and now the moment had been lost. And not just lost. She had the depressing feeling it would never come again.

'Mr Maitland's results are back from the lab,' Jane said the minute she saw Robert, 'and you'll be pleased to know it's negative on the meningitis. Looks like he's simply got a very bad case of the flu, but do you want me to arrange for him to go up to the medical ward for observation?'

Robert nodded.

'A successful birth, and a good result for Mr Maitland,' Hannah declared. 'Hey, maybe this is going to be one of our better days.'

'Never, *ever* say that, Hannah,' Jane protested in dismay. 'The minute anyone says that in A and E, you can be sure the floodgates will open.'

And they did. Within half an hour the waiting room was packed, and Robert and Hannah were desperately attempting to extract information from a very drowsy and equally belligerent overdose patient.

'Why don't you just go away and leave me alone?' the woman flared as Robert tried to find out what pills she'd taken. 'I don't want you to help me! I just want to die!'

'Won't you at least tell us when you took the pills?' Hannah said coaxingly. 'Was it an hour ago—two hours—longer?'

'Sod off, why don't you?' the woman retorted. 'Just sod off, and leave me alone!'

'Alcohol as well as pills, from the smell of her breath,' Robert observed. 'Can't whoever brought her in give us any information?'

Jane shook her head. 'All her boyfriend knows is that they had a huge row last night and when he went round to their flat to collect his clothes he found her in the bathroom, clutching an empty pill bottle.'

'Which he didn't think to bring in with him.' Robert sighed. 'OK, Jane, get me a sample for a blood alcohol level, a toxic screen to identify what she's taken and a CBC and ECG. If she's taken any of the tricyclic antidepressants they can play havoc with the heart rhythm.'

'Are you going to try to make her vomit?' Hannah asked, knowing that they couldn't wait for the results of any of the tests Robert had ordered but had to immediately attempt to prevent the digestion and absorption of any pills the woman had taken.

Robert shook his head. 'God only knows when she took her overdose, and if she took it more than two hours ago any pills will already be in her intestines and making her vomit won't help at all.'

Which meant they would have to use the tube. It was an unpleasant and uncomfortable enough procedure on a patient who wanted to be helped, but on someone who decided to fight them it proved to be a nightmare.

'Leave me alone!' she shrieked, lashing out with her hands and feet as Jane tried to insert the tube into her mouth. 'I don't want you to help me. I want to die. Do you hear me? I *want* to die!'

'I know you do, but I'm afraid we're not going to let you,' Robert said grimly, clasping hold of her arms. 'Keep going, Jane, Hannah.'

It was easier said than done, Hannah thought wryly as she and Jane tried to ease the tube into the woman's mouth, down through her oesophagus and into her stomach. It was like dealing with a writhing eel, a writhing eel with lethal flailing feet as she soon discovered when one caught her in the stomach and sent her flying back against the cubicle wall to land in an undignified heap on the floor.

'Are you OK, Hannah?' Robert demanded with concern.

Gingerly she got to her feet and rubbed her bottom. 'A case of hurt dignity, that's all.'

'You're sure?' he insisted, but when she nodded he turned to the woman on the trolley, his face grim. 'Now listen to me, and listen good. We're going to get those pills out of you whether you like it or not. If you choose to do something stupid like this again after you're discharged, that's your prerogative, but at the moment you are in our care and we are damned well going to help you, whether you want it or not!'

Whether his outburst had stunned her or whether the woman had just grown tired of fighting them was unclear, but she didn't say another word as Jane and Hannah slipped the tube down into her stomach and began the unpleasant task of sucking up any pill fragments.

And it was unpleasant. Not only did they have to suction the remnants of the pills away, they then had to clean out the woman's stomach by pouring water down the tube followed by a slush of charcoal to absorb any remaining medication.

'What will happen to her now?' Hannah asked when the results from the lab confirmed that, though their patient had taken Valium mixed with alcohol, her CBC was fine.

'We'll send her up to IC to ensure she doesn't slip into respiratory or cardiac failure,' Robert replied, stripping off his latex gloves and binning them. 'Once they're happy with her she'll be referred to a psychiatric ward for evaluation.'

Hannah sighed as she watched the woman being wheeled out of the treatment room. 'It must be truly awful to feel your life isn't worth living.'

'Yes.'

She glanced round at him quickly. His answer had been low, scarcely audible, and his face was dark, shadowed. Did he feel that way, too? Had he loved his wife so much that he felt his own life wasn't worth living?

'Robert—'

He was already walking away from her, and as she stared after him she couldn't help a wistful sigh escaping from her—a sigh she speedily smothered when she heard Elliot's deep chuckle behind her.

'Really smitten, aren't you, love?'

Hot colour flooded her cheeks. 'I don't know what you're talking about.'

'Yeah, and my other leg's got bells on it!' he exclaimed. 'Does he know how you feel?'

For a second she considered lying, but Elliot was a friend, a good friend, and whatever else he was he most certainly wasn't a gossip. 'I don't think he even knows I exist.' She sighed.

'You really think that?' he said in surprise.

She nodded sadly. 'I'm the kid. Little Miss Muffet.'

'Little Miss Muffet?' Elliot repeated, bewildered.

'It's a long story, Elliot. Let's just say I know what I'm talking about.'

'Hannah, I don't think you do. In fact—'

'RTA on the way, folks!' Mary on Reception called urgently from the office door. 'Mother and three kids. The kids look to be in the worse shape!'

They were, and once Mr Mackay and Robert had stabilised them sufficiently to be moved, they were immediately sent off by ambulance to the Royal Sick Children's where they would receive more specialist care.

'Mrs Ogilvie seems to have got off amazingly lightly—just cuts and bruises,' Hannah observed when Robert joined her outside cubicle 8. 'I've got her on an IV line to counteract the possible effects of shock, and Jane's linked her to the ECG machine as a precaution.'

'Good work.' He nodded approvingly. 'Any sign of chest damage from the steering-wheel?'

'None at all. Like I said, when you consider her car skidded straight into a wall, she's had a miraculous escape. How are her children? She keeps asking about them, and I've been fobbing her off.'

'Keep on fobbing her off. The last I heard they were all stable, but things can change very fast, and the less stress she has to bear at the moment the better.'

Hannah nodded. 'Apparently she was driving her children over to her mother's for the afternoon. Has anyone telephoned Mrs Ludlow yet? According to Gwen Ogilvie, Grandma gets panicky if they're even ten minutes late—'

'Hannah—Robert!' Jane suddenly yelled from inside the cubicle. 'I've got no pulse!'

No pulse? Hannah's eyes flew to Robert's. But that meant…that meant…

Without a word they dashed through the cubicle curtains. Jane had already started CPR and swiftly Hannah and Robert inserted an endotracheal tube. They had to get Gwen's heart beating again, but first they had to make sure that sufficient oxygen was reaching her brain.

'Ventilator linked—still no BP or pulse!' Jane announced, her face grim.

'Epi. push intravenously,' Robert demanded, and the moment the epinephrine was added to the IV line he picked up the defibrillator paddles. 'OK, everyone stand clear!'

Obediently Jane and Hannah stepped back from the trolley and quickly Robert placed the paddles on Gwen Ogilvie's chest. Her body arched and convulsed as the electricity surged through her body, but the ECG monitor remained resolutely flat.

'Lidocaine!' he called.

The drug was swiftly added to the IV line, then they all stepped away from the trolley again as Robert upped the voltage on the defibrillator to 360.

It didn't do any good. Nothing did any good. They gave Gwen Ogilvie every drug at their disposal to try to kick-start her heart, but still nothing happened, and eventually Robert switched off the defibrillator and threw down the paddles.

'OK, that's it, folks,' he muttered. 'We gave it our best shot, but...' He glanced across at Hannah who was staring down at Gwen Ogilvie's inert body. 'Are you OK, Hannah?'

'Yes...yes, of course I am,' she replied.

She wasn't. Robert could see very well she wasn't. There was a dazed, disbelieving look about her eyes, the look all junior doctors wore when they encountered their first failure, and his heart went out to her.

'Hannah, listen...' He paused and frowned. All too clearly he could hear the sound of their receptionist outside in the treatment room, pleading, cajoling, and the sound of a man's raised voice angrily, arguing back. 'What the hell's going on out there?'

Hannah neither knew nor cared, but she obediently followed him out of the cubicle, to find their receptionist desperately attempting to restrain a young man in his mid-thirties.

'Robert, I'm sorry, but I couldn't stop him,' the receptionist said, her cheeks red, her eyes apologetic. 'It's Eric Ogilvie—Gwen Ogilvie's husband.'

Robert nodded. 'Perhaps you'd like to come with me to one of our waiting rooms, Mr Ogilvie—'

'But the police said you have my wife here,' Eric Ogilvie interrupted, throwing off Robert's hand as he tried to steer him towards the door. 'Where is she? I want to see her!'

'Of course you do,' Robert said quietly, gently but firmly clasping Mr Ogilvie's arm again and motioning to Hannah that she should accompany them. 'I just need to talk to you first.'

And he did. With an understanding and sympathy that brought a hard lump to Hannah's throat, he explained what had happened.

'But you said she wasn't hurt in the crash. He did say

that, didn't he?' Eric said, his eyes swivelling round to Hannah in mute appeal.

'We don't know why she suffered a heart attack,' she said softly. There would be time enough later to tell him there'd have to be a post-mortem. 'Perhaps there was a weakness, and the shock of the accident—'

'But she was always so fit,' Eric protested. 'Never a day's illness. Are you sure you've got the right Gwen Ogilvie? She's small, blonde, with a tiny scar on her left cheek. She fell off a garden swing, you see, when she was six, and it's very distinctive—'

'It *is* your wife, Mr Ogilvie,' Robert said gently. 'Look, is there anyone we can call for you—a relative who could come—?'

'I was supposed to drive the kids over to their grandma this afternoon, but I've got this really lousy cold, and Gwen…' Eric shook his head as though to clear it 'We had a bit of a row before she left—she was worried in case she'd be late for her appointment with the obstetrician.'

'The obstetrician?' Hannah repeated, her heart sinking.

'She's pregnant, three months pregnant. We're hoping it's going to be a girl this time. I suppose I ought to phone—cancel the appointment. Doctors don't like to be kept hanging about, do they? And—'

'Mr Ogilvie—'

'You're sure it's her?' Eric interrupted. 'She's small, you know, with blonde hair and a little scar down the left hand side of her cheek. There must be hundreds of Gwen Ogilvies in the world. It would be so easy to make a mistake…to…to get the wrong girl…'

He was crying now, low strangled sobs that were convulsing his whole frame, and Hannah went to him quickly. She'd never heard a man cry before, never seen one cry, and the worst of it was that there was nothing she could do but hold his shaking body and wish, like Eric Ogilvie, that it had all been a terrible mistake.

She got through the rest of the afternoon on autopilot. I'm fine, she kept telling herself as she sounded people's chests, listened to their symptoms and patched them up as best she could. I'm a doctor, I can cope with this, she kept repeating like a mantra, and wished that somehow she could make herself believe it, and that the hard, cold lump around her heart would go away.

Never had a shift seemed so endless. Never had her nerves felt quite so strained to breaking point, and when she noticed Jerry Clark walking down the corridor towards her as she came out of A and E's small dispensary, she strode on past him without a word.

'Hey, cat got your tongue, beautiful?' he called after her, but when she didn't even pause he hurried after her. 'I hear you had a bit of an accident earlier this afternoon. Fell on your cute little butt, so I hear.'

'I'm busy—'

'We all are, sweetheart, but I just wanted you to know that if you need someone to kiss it better, I'll be only too happy to oblige.'

He was smiling at her with that smile which always made her want to scrub herself down with disinfectant, smirking like some sniggering schoolboy poring over a dirty magazine, and suddenly something snapped inside her.

'Quite frankly, I wouldn't let you kiss the floor I walked on!' she exclaimed, her face white with anger. 'In fact, I'd prefer not to even breathe the same air as you do in future!'

His jaw dropped. 'Hey, it was a joke, Hannah—'

'My name is *Dr Blake*,' she interrupted, unaware that her voice was rising in pitch. 'And let me tell you this. If you don't stop your crass attempts at flirtation, which are as unwelcome as they are revolting, I'm going straight to the head of Human Resources to file an official complaint against you!'

Jerry's eyes narrowed into small slits. 'Now, hold on there a minute Miss High-and-Mighty Blake. There's such a thing as slander—'

'And there's such a thing as sexual harassment, Jerry,' Robert said icily, appearing without warning at the end of the corridor, his face tight. 'I suggest you think about that— think long and hard. Hannah, I need to talk to you in the staffroom if you can spare the time.'

'Talk to me?' she murmured, gazing up at him, bemused and bewildered. 'But I have patients to see. You have patients—'

'And Elliot can manage for a few minutes without us,' he declared, propelling her inexorably towards the staffroom, but by the time they'd reached it she'd already guessed what he wanted to say.

'Robert, you don't need to tell me that I shouldn't have lost my temper—that I should have gone through official channels—'

'Official channels be damned.' He smiled. 'I'd have happily held your coat for you if you'd wanted to sock him.'

'But—'

'Hannah, he had it coming, and if it's any help I'll make damn sure that Radiology sends us a different technician in future.'

'You can do that?' she said faintly.

'You bet your life I can,' he replied. 'In fact, I can personally rearrange Jerry's not so charming features for you if you want, and take the greatest pleasure in doing it.'

She chuckled a little shakily. 'I don't think that's a good idea. In fact, I know it's not, but I appreciate the offer.'

He stared at her thoughtfully for a second, then sat down. 'You could have had this out with Jerry weeks ago. Why now? Why lose your temper now?'

She picked up one of the dog-eared magazines on the coffee-table, then put it down again. 'I guess...I guess he just caught me on the raw. It's been one of those days, you know? I was really worried about doing Mr Maitland's spinal tap, then that lovely baby arrived, and...'

'Gwen Ogilvie,' he finished for her gently.

She didn't want to talk about Gwen Ogilvie. She'd spent the whole afternoon determinedly not thinking about Gwen Ogilvie, but suddenly the words started tumbling jerkily out of her.

'I was talking to her before you arrived. She was telling me all about her children, the schools they went to, how Duncan—that's her eldest boy—was becoming really cheeky and she was getting worried about him. We were talking just like two ordinary, normal people, and then...and then...'

'Hannah—'

'Why, Robert? *Why?*' She hiccuped as the hard lump around her heart cracked, and tears began to spill down her cheeks despite her best efforts to prevent them. 'She wasn't much older than me. She had so much to live for—her husband, her children, the new baby coming. Why did she have to die when other people—horrible, dreadful people—survive?'

'I don't know.'

The admission sounded as though it had been dragged from somewhere deep inside him and her eyes flew to his face with horror. His wife. How could she have forgotten that his wife had died in St Stephen's after a road accident? That he'd been on duty when they'd brought her in?

'Oh, God, I'm sorry—so sorry!' she gasped, dragging a hand roughly across her wet cheeks. 'And I accused Jerry of crassness—of insensitivity. Your wife—Laura...'

'It's all right, Hannah.'

'No, it's not!' she protested. 'It isn't all right. I should have thought. Every time an RTA comes in, you must remember, it must bring it all back.'

It did, but not in the way Hannah meant. Oh, he remembered the impotence he'd felt as he'd watched Laura slipping away from him despite all his skill. The rage he'd felt at her dying. But most of all he remembered the guilt. The unbearable guilt of knowing she would still have been alive if it hadn't been for him. She would still have been alive if he hadn't married her and discovered it had been a huge mistake, then demanded a divorce.

'I'm so sorry, Robert,' Hannah said again, and he saw the sympathy in her large brown eyes and couldn't bear it.

He didn't want her sympathy, he deserved none. It was his fault Laura was dead. His fault she was lying in that cold grave.

But as he continued to stare at Hannah he realised something else. It wasn't simply sympathy he saw in her eyes. There was love there, too. Love and need. A love and need he knew he felt as well, despite all his attempts to deny it, and his heart contracted with pain.

He didn't want to fall in love again. He didn't want this lovely, vulnerable girl to be in love with him. He'd hurt her as he'd hurt Laura—he knew he would—and because he knew that, he determinedly forced a careless, dismissive smile to his face.

'Far worse things have happened to other people. I'll survive.'

'But you must miss her dreadfully,' she murmured, her eyes still shimmering with unshed tears.

'Good heavens, no,' he replied with a casual negligence that tore at his heart. 'It happened over a year ago, and there's no sense or point in wallowing in grief.'

The sympathy that had been in her eyes was instantly replaced by shock and disapproval. Which was exactly

what he'd wanted, he told himself as she blew her nose
and hastily made her excuses.

Only a fool wouldn't have learned from bitter experience. Only a fool would let his heart rule his head. And if
he felt something wither and die inside him as she disappeared out of the staffroom without a backward glance, it
was for the best. Better for her to be hurt now than later.
Far, far better.

CHAPTER EIGHT

'I SHOULDN'T laugh—I really, really shouldn't,' Hannah said, 'but—'

'You can't think of anyone who looks less like Superman?' Floella suggested, her lips twitching, as they watched their portly patient being wheeled out of the treatment room, the remnants of his Superman costume lying in pieces at his feet.

Hannah nodded unsteadily. 'The poor man. He was trying so hard to be romantic for his wife's birthday, and now he's going to be in traction for weeks with that slipped disc.'

'His wife didn't think it was particularly romantic,' Jane observed, her grey eyes dancing. 'Not when he got stuck halfway between the roof of their garden shed and bedroom with that box of chocolates in his mouth.'

'And the fire brigade didn't think it was very romantic either when they had to rescue him,' Floella gurgled. 'In fact, they said it was the best laugh they'd had in years. The poor man's never going to live it down. He'll probably have to move house, leave town—'

'And if you three have got nothing better to do than stand around gossiping all evening, perhaps Mr Mackay and I should take a long hard look at our staffing requirements!' Robert snapped as he strode past them.

Hannah bit her lip, Jane flushed crimson and Floella spluttered with indignation as Robert disappeared into the office.

'I've had it!' she exclaimed. 'I really have had it! I know he's always expected high standards from us—and quite

133

right, too—and I know he has a quick temper, but these last two weeks have been impossible. You only have to smile and you get your head bitten off!'

'And I was beginning to think he didn't look quite so stressed,' Jane sighed. 'That he was starting to ease up on his workload, but...'

'Someone is going to have to talk to him,' Floella said firmly. 'Working in A and E is hard enough, without having to tiptoe around your special reg, especially when you haven't got the faintest idea why you're tiptoeing around him in the first place!'

Hannah nodded absently, only to suddenly realise that two pairs of eyes were fixed expectantly on her. 'Oh, no— no way—not me! I'm just the junior doctor, the new kid on the block.'

'Yes, but he likes you,' Jane urged. 'In fact, you're the only person he hasn't been appallingly rude to recently.'

'Give him time,' Hannah said ruefully. 'Look, if you're so worried about him, why don't you speak to Mr Mackay, the department consultant? He's the boss—'

'And about as much use for something like this as a wet flannel,' Floella said. 'You'd be so much better, Hannah. He likes you, as Jane said, and—'

'No,' Hannah interrupted firmly. 'I'm sorry, but there's no way I'm going to talk to him—no way!'

And she couldn't, she thought as she walked quickly down the treatment room. How could she speak to a man who was doing his level best to avoid her? How could she possibly have any kind of conversation with someone who spent the whole time fidgeting with his watch, examining his tie and looking everywhere but at her?

And it had been like that ever since Gwen Ogilvie's death. Since he'd told her, quite callously and dismissively, that he never thought about his wife.

She didn't believe him. Oh, she'd been shocked and horrified at the time, but the more she'd thought about it, the more she'd become convinced that he'd deliberately set out to make her think the worst of him.

And yet why in the world would anyone want to do that? It didn't make any sense. In fact, nothing about Robert Cunningham made sense at the moment, she thought in confusion, turning in answer to Jane's urgent call.

'RTA on the way, Hannah! ETA, five minutes, and it looks like a bad one!'

It was. In fact, it was by far the worst road accident Hannah had ever seen.

'How on earth did that happen?' she said with horror as the paramedics carefully transferred their casualty onto the examination trolley and she saw the two-foot steel bar imbedded in his chest.

'Mr Ingram was on his way to collect his kid from a Hallowe'en party when he hit some ice on the motorway and collided with the crash barriers,' one of the paramedics replied. 'His seat belt snapped, he went straight through the windscreen—'

'And part of the crash barrier ended up imbedded in his chest,' Robert finished grimly as he, Floella and Jane joined them. 'What's his GCS?'

'Two-two-five.'

A score of 8 or lower on the Glasgow coma scale meant you had very serious injuries indeed and, at 9, Trevor Ingram was much too close for comfort. There was no way they could remove the metal bar—that was a job for the operating-theatre staff—but if they didn't stabilise him quickly, the young man wouldn't even reach the theatre.

'Intubation?' Hannah declared, immediately reaching for an endotracheal tube to replace the ambu-bag the paramedics had been using, but Robert shook his head.

'Not with those facial injuries. I doubt if you'd be able to see clearly enough into his mouth to be sure of getting the tube down his throat and into his trachea. I'll have to do a crike.'

A cricothyrotomy. A delicate and precise procedure which involved making a vertical incision into the throat, followed by a horizontal cut into the cricothyroid membrane. A breathing tube was then inserted into the hole and attached to the ventilator, but in inexperienced hands a lot could go wrong. You could put the tube in the wrong place, even sever one of the big arteries in the oesophagus, and if you did that then your patient was in mega-trouble.

'BP dropping,' Floella warned after Robert had performed the cricothyrotomy, making the whole procedure look like child's play. 'Sixty over forty.'

'And he doesn't seem to have any breath sounds on the right side,' Hannah advised, listening carefully to Trevor Ingram's chest through her stethoscope.

Air was seeping into the young man's chest with every breath he took but it wasn't going out again, and a large bubble of air was compressing the collapsed lung on his right side. Unless they relieved the tension pneumothorax, Trevor Ingram's heart, and the great blood vessels surrounding it, would eventually become so compressed that no pumping action would be possible, and no blood would reach his brain.

'ECG status, Jane?' Robert demanded.

'Jumping around a bit, but not worryingly so.'

He nodded and quickly stabbed a needle into the young man's chest. The trapped air was released almost immediately, but though Trevor's trachea started to shift back to the middle of his neck, a chest tube would have to be inserted to help re-expand his lung.

'O-negative up and running, Robert,' Floella called.

'OK, get me a CBC, urine sample and guiac test. I'll want chest, neck and pelvis X-rays as well. Hannah—chest tube, please.'

Did he mean she was to insert it? It certainly looked that way, and carefully she made a small incision into Trevor Ingram's chest down into the lining around his lung. With equal care she then inserted the tube, which would suck out the blood and air and eventually reinflate the young man's lung.

'BP rising,' Jane announced, 'but we can't get the IVs in, Robert. His veins won't take them.'

Robert swore under his breath. Without IV lines to provide the fluids needed to temporarily replace the blood Trevor Ingram was losing, there was no way they could support his blood pressure while they attempted to bring his bleeding under control.

'I'm going to have to go for a central line directly into the internal subclavian veins in his neck,' Robert declared.

It required great skill to do that without hitting a major artery, but with an ease Hannah could only admire Robert soon had the central line inserted.

God, he was good, she thought enviously. Nothing threw him, nothing disturbed him. OK, so perhaps he'd been a little—all right, then, very—difficult to work with lately, but he was still the best special registrar in the business. And the kindest, she added mentally as Craig Larkin arrived to take the X-rays they needed.

Robert had been as good as his word about contacting Radiology to tell them Jerry Clark was no longer welcome in A and E. Craig Larkin had taken his place the very next day—calm, efficient and utterly professional—and he was now an accepted member of the team. What Jerry thought of the change was anybody's guess, and Hannah neither knew nor cared.

But she did care about the man standing opposite her, oblivious to everything apart from the patient in his charge. Cared deeply and desperately, but from the distant way he'd been treating her since Gwen Ogilvie's death she'd been forced to come to the depressing conclusion that her feelings weren't reciprocated.

'No blood in the urine or guiac test, Robert,' Jane declared, 'and the CBC results suggest we're winning.'

They were when Floella finally announced Trevor Ingram's BP was 95 over 60.

It wasn't a wonderful blood pressure, but at least it meant they'd stabilised him sufficiently to be sent to the operating theatre where the difficult task of removing the metal bar from his chest could begin.

'Well done, everybody,' Robert said, pulling off his latex gloves and running his fingers through his damp hair. 'That was good work.'

It was. Good, united teamwork. The kind of work Hannah had always dreamt, hoped, she'd be a part of and, though she felt completely drained, she felt elated, too.

'Do you think he'll make it, Robert?' she asked as Trevor Ingram was wheeled out of the treatment room, the IV bags swinging above him.

'It all depends upon what they find when they remove the steel bar,' he said, rubbing the back of his neck wearily. 'I hope he makes it. After what he's been through, he certainly deserves to.'

'If I'd been through what he has, I'd want to keep a part of that crash barrier as a souvenir,' she observed.

'If it were me I'd have it mounted permanently on my dashboard as a reminder to slow down the next time there's icy weather,' he replied.

She chuckled, and for a second—an infinitesimal second—saw the beginnings of an answering smile curve his lips. Then it was gone.

'Right— Yes, well, this certainly isn't getting on with the work,' he declared brusquely, and before she could say a word he walked away, leaving her gazing unhappily after him.

Was this how it was going to be from now on? Conversations limited to a simple 'yes' or a 'no' unless it was something to do with work? Shared smiles out of the question because they suggested a familiarity and friendship that didn't exist?

It had all been so different two weeks ago when little Miss No Name had been born. Then she'd felt a closeness to him, a bond she'd believed he felt as well, and yet now...

Now she would infinitely have preferred Robert to have been as sharp with her as he was with everyone else in the department. At least it would have been better than this cool distancing. At least it would have shown he recognised she was alive, that she was there.

'I take it things aren't going well in the romance stakes?' Elliot murmured softly as he joined her.

'You could say that,' she replied through a throat so tight it hurt.

The SHO sighed. 'Well, all I can say is the guy needs his head examined.'

'I think maybe I'm the one who should be having that done, don't you?' she replied sadly.

'You're far too good for him—he doesn't deserve you,' Elliot declared stoutly. 'In fact, I never could understand what you saw in him in the first place, especially when there was someone like me around.'

She blew her nose and managed a watery smile. 'So you're on offer, are you?'

'I could be if I thought you'd be even remotely interested.' He smiled, and if his smile didn't quite reach his eyes she never noticed. 'Robert *is* in love with you, you know. He may not realise yet—or perhaps want to admit it...'

'So you've got the second sight now, have you?' She couldn't help but chuckle.

'Absolutely,' he replied, his mouth turning up at the corners. 'Not to mention also being modest, shy, retiring—'

'And soon to be made redundant if you don't get back to work!' Robert exclaimed as he strode past them and into cubicle 6.

For a moment Elliot said nothing, then he turned to Hannah, his face rueful. 'All I can say is if he doesn't face up to the fact that he's besotted with you soon, he won't have a member of staff left who's still speaking to him.'

She bit her lip. 'Elliot, it isn't me. I wish it was, but it's not. I don't know what's wrong with him, but his bad temper's got nothing to do with me.'

'If you say so, love,' he said. 'But in the meantime I'm afraid it's back to the grindstone, and roll on eleven o'clock.'

Hannah heartily wished it was eleven o'clock, too, by the time she'd finished examining her next patient—a tiny, frail-looking eighty-five-year-old—who despite her apparent fragility had managed in the space of fifteen minutes to comment adversely on her hairstyle, clothes and medical abilities.

'Boy, but is she a real charmer,' Floella muttered as she collected the blood samples Hannah had asked for.

'To be fair, she has very bad arthritis in her hands and feet, which probably doesn't do a lot for her temper,' Hannah murmured back, determined to be charitable, then frowned. 'Reception said she had a suspected fractured leg, didn't they?'

Floella nodded. 'According to her son, she fell in the house just before dinner, and he's worried she might have broken her leg.'

There hadn't been a single bruise on the old woman's leg, neither had she complained of any pain when Hannah had examined her. She'd complained about everything else, but not about pain in her leg.

'Flo, could you go out to the waiting room and check with her son again? Maybe he's given Reception the wrong information. It's very easily done when someone's upset.'

Floella was back within seconds, her face furious. 'We've been had, Hannah. It's a granny drop!'

'A what?' Hannah said in confusion.

'The classic answer of what to do with Grandma or Grandad when you decide to take a holiday,' the sister replied bitterly. 'If you're too mean to spend money on a home help or a hotel, you simply drive to the nearest A and E and drop the problem off.'

'I don't believe it!' Hannah gasped.

'Neither will Robert when he finds out we've been conned,' Floella groaned. 'He'll have to phone Geriatrics to see if they can find her a bed, and by the time they've finished giving him merry hell he'll want our guts for garters.'

He did. Or, more precisely, he wanted Hannah's.

'How could you have been so stupid?' he demanded, angrily stabbing his hands through his black hair. 'Falling for a scam like that. It's one of the oldest tricks in the book!'

'In which case you should have warned me and I'd have been prepared,' she protested.

'Do you have to be told everything?' he snapped. 'Can't you use whatever little brain and common sense you've got and figure some things out for yourself?'

Well, she'd wanted him to be rude to her, she remembered, but that didn't mean she had to like it, and she discovered she didn't—not at all.

'And just how—exactly—am I supposed to predict which sons are going to dump their mothers on us?' she retorted.

'Perhaps if you weren't so damned naïve—'

'I'd rather be naïve than a complete cynic like you!' she

threw back at him. 'Look, I made a mistake, OK? I'm sorry, OK? What do you want from me—blood?'

What he wanted, he realised, looking down at her flushed cheeks and furious eyes, was to kiss her senseless. What he really wanted was to take her to bed and make love to her.

Why couldn't he just fall out of love with her? He'd fallen out of love with Laura, so why couldn't he do the same with Hannah? Hell, he'd tried hard enough. Keeping out of her way, exchanging the barest minimum of conversation with her—but it hadn't worked.

All he felt was lousier than before. Lousy, and frustrated, and angry. Angry with her for making him feel this way. Angry with himself for being stupid enough to have fallen in love again. And angry with everybody else because...because... Well, he didn't know why he was angry with everybody else. He just knew that he was.

'What I want, Dr Blake, is for you to shape up your ideas,' he said tightly. And to stop wearing that damn perfume you always wear. The one that smells of bluebells and daffodils. To stop looking at me with those big brown eyes of yours, all hurt, and baffled, and confused. 'What I want is you to start behaving in a professional manner!'

'A professional manner?' she repeated. 'You have the nerve—the *gall*—to suggest that because I was conned by that old lady's son I'm not *professional*?'

Of course he hadn't meant that, but there was no way he was going to explain to her what he really meant. And to his relief he didn't have to. As he cleared his throat to reply, the doors of the treatment room suddenly clattered open and a wild-eyed, panic-stricken girl appeared, with a baby in her arms.

'Please—please, will somebody help me? My son... My baby's not breathing properly!'

The tiny mite was almost blue, his chest was caving in

with the effort to breathe, and together Robert and Hannah rushed towards him, their argument immediately forgotten.

'How old is he?' Hannah asked, taking the child from his mother's arms and quickly carrying him into one of the cubicles.

'Two weeks old. He was born two weeks ago.'

A premature baby for sure, Hannah decided, placing her stethoscope swiftly onto its little chest. A full-term baby wouldn't have been nearly so small and fragile, and though the poor little mite had obviously been crying, he wasn't crying now. All of his tiny energies were concentrated on simply trying to breathe.

'How long has your son been like this?' Robert asked, quickly setting up a tiny drip and linking the baby to the ECG monitor.

'Two—maybe three days.'

Robert's eyes met Hannah's. Three *days*? What kind of mother allowed her child to suffer like this for three days? Judging by his temperature, the baby probably had a massive infection of some kind, and leaving him without medical treatment for even three hours was far too long.

They could stabilise his condition—in fact, the drip Robert had inserted was already improving the baby's colour and breathing—but the special care baby unit was the best place for him, and that was where he would go after they'd extracted as much information out of the mother as they could.

'Was it a normal birth?' Hannah asked as she took the baby's blood pressure.

'I think so,' the girl replied uncertainly. 'I mean, I've never had a baby before, so I can't really say whether it was any different to anyone else's labour.'

'What Dr Blake meant was did the midwife notice anything unusual when your son was born?' Robert asked.

'Jaundice perhaps, or breathing problems, anything like that?'

The girl frowned. 'Not that I recall, though they did say they'd found amphetamines in his body when he was born.'

And how do you suppose the amphetamines got there, you stupid girl? Hannah fumed. You put them in him. You must have been pill-popping when you were pregnant, and now your son is suffering because of it.

But she didn't say that. Never judge, she'd been taught at med school, never criticise. You're a doctor whose primary function is to heal, but to her dismay it soon became apparent that Robert had already judged and he was going to announce his verdict whether the young girl wanted to hear it or not.

'I presume you went to antenatal classes?' he demanded.

'I went once or twice,' the girl said, 'but it was such a hassle getting there—'

'Then you presumably missed the talk about how everything you put in your mouth would go straight into your baby's body!' he said caustically. 'Your son has breathing difficulties because he was born a drug addict. Your son has a fever because he's suffering from withdrawal symptoms.'

'Dr Cunningham, I really don't think this is perhaps the best time—'

'Your baby is going to have to do cold turkey because of your irresponsibility,' Robert continued as though Hannah hadn't spoken, his eyes fixed icily on the baby's mother. 'His little body is going to be racked with pain and agony because of you, and I hope when you sit by his incubator and hear his tiny screams that you remember that!'

And before Hannah could stop him he had swung out of the cubicle, leaving her staring after him in stunned horror. Never had she seen Robert come so close to completely losing his temper before. OK, so what he'd told the baby's mother was true. And, OK, the girl was obviously clueless, but a cubicle in the middle of A and E was hardly the proper place or the right time to tell her so.

'I'm...I'm so very sorry,' she said awkwardly as the girl began to cry. 'Dr Cunningham...he's been under a lot of strain recently, and I can only apologise for his...his brusqueness.'

And get you and your baby up to SCBU as fast as I can, she added mentally, quickly poking her head round the cubicle curtains to find Elliot, Jane and Floella standing outside, their faces concerned and worried.

'Oh, Hannah, this really can't go on, you know,' Jane said, lowering her voice as the members of the night shift began to arrive. 'It's one thing to be snippy with us, but—'

'We're here to treat, not to judge,' Elliot finished for her. 'Hannah, he was completely out of order.'

'I know that, but—'

'Won't you at least try to talk to him?' Jane continued as Hannah gazed at her unhappily. 'You could do it tonight. You could go round to his flat, speak to him privately...'

'But, Jane—'

'What if he does something worse tomorrow?' the sister declared. 'Hannah, he's the best special registrar I've ever worked with, and...well, I know he's got his faults, but I'm worried sick about him.'

Hannah was too, which was why she found herself standing on the doorstep of Robert's flat some time later, pale and nervous but utterly determined.

'So little Miss Muffet is doing house calls now, is she?' he commented coldly when he opened the door and saw her. 'Well, I'm sorry to disappoint you, but I don't believe I need your medical services tonight.'

And to her dismay he actually began to shut the door on her.

'OK, we can have this conversation on the doorstep for all your neighbours to hear,' she said grimly, quickly putting her foot in the doorway and keeping it there. 'Or you can invite me in to listen to what I have to say like a civilised human being.'

For a second she thought he really was going to make her say it on the doorstep but then, without a word, he turned on his heel and strode down the hall, leaving her to follow him.

And she did, into what had to be the most cheerless sitting room she'd ever seen. Oh, it was nicely furnished if your taste ran to the basic, and spotlessly neat, but it wasn't a home. Homes had clutter. Homes had ornaments and photographs, and books and magazines lying where people had left them. This room had all the charm of one of those huge corporate hotels. Anonymous, functional and completely soulless.

'Oh, for God's sake, will you stop hovering over me like some student nurse checking out her first patient?' he exclaimed irritably as he sat down. 'Take a seat, say what you've got to say, then I'd be obliged if you'd leave and allow me to enjoy what remains of my evening in peace.'

Now was the moment to tell him that it was scathing comments like that which were putting everybody's backs up, but the words wouldn't come, and it wasn't because she'd suddenly got a bad attack of cold feet. It was because he looked so lost somehow, sitting in this soulless, cheerless flat, with nothing but his memories for company.

'Robert…I'm here because everyone's so worried about you—'

'What you mean is everyone's had enough of my bad temper, and you were unlucky enough to draw the short straw to tell me so,' he flared.

She coloured slightly. 'In a way I guess that's so, but we *are* worried about you. That girl and her baby…'

'I went too far—I admit it,' he exclaimed. 'I'll go up to SCBU tomorrow and apologise to her. Happy now?'

No, she wasn't, not by a long shot. 'Robert, we all know you're unhappy, and we want to help you. We know how much you loved your wife—'

'Do you remember me telling you once that we should trade secrets?' he interrupted. 'That I would tell you why I intended to get blind drunk on the anniversary of my wife's death if you would tell me why you took a job in London instead of Edinburgh?'

She shifted uneasily in her seat. Now wasn't the right time to tell him about her father. She didn't know when that would be, but it certainly wasn't now. 'Robert—'

'Well, I'll tell you for free,' he continued, his face bleak, empty. 'I wanted to get drunk that night because I killed her. I killed Laura.'

Her eyes flew to his face in confusion. 'But she was hit by a car outside the hospital—'

'And she wouldn't have been if she hadn't left St Stephen's so angry that the last thing she was thinking about was road safety,' he said bitterly. 'We'd had a row—a huge one—and I...I told her I wanted a divorce. If she hadn't been angry with me that night, she would still be alive. I killed her, Hannah. I might not have been driving the car, but I still killed her.'

She didn't know what to say, but she knew she had to say something. 'You said you had a row...?'

'The last of far too many,' he murmured, leaning back in his seat and closing his eyes. 'Laura...Laura was by far the most gifted doctor I've ever met, and it never occurred to me to look beyond that. To see that the only thing she really cared for wasn't me, or her patients, but her work and the success it could bring.'

'But surely she must have loved you if she married you?' Hannah protested.

'I think…I think she loved me as much as she was capable of loving anyone, but I wanted more, you see. I wanted to be the most important thing in her life, and she couldn't give me that. Maybe I was selfish, unrealistic. Maybe I wanted too much, but…' His lips twisted. 'Oh, Hannah, you can have no idea what it's like to live with someone—to love them deeply, desperately—and yet to know that you only ever occupy a tiny, unimportant part of their heart.'

But she did know, she thought as the memories came flooding back.

Memories of herself as a child, sitting up well past her bedtime waiting for her father to come home from the hospital. Longing to see him, to talk to him, to have him cuddle and hold her. And of her father coming home and absently patting her on the head before he disappeared into his study to plan his next big operation.

'Robert—'

'Would you tell the others I appreciate their concern for my career, and apologise to them for my recent behaviour?' he interrupted quickly. 'Tell them…' He managed a smile. 'Tell them I'll try to do better in future.'

There was nothing left to say. She'd done what she'd been asked to do, and slowly she got to her feet, and even more slowly walked over to the sitting-room door, but when she reached it she turned to face him.

'It wasn't your career we were concerned about, you know. We care a great deal for you. Jane, and Flo, and Elliot, and…me.'

'Hannah—'

'In fact…' She took a deep breath and threw all caution to the wind. 'I more than care, Robert. I—'

'Don't!' he interrupted, springing to his feet. 'Don't—please, don't say it.'

'Why not?' she asked, her heart beginning to beat very fast. 'Why don't you want me to say it?'

'Because you and I... Hannah, I've thought and thought about this, and I do want you—I won't deny it—but it would never work.'

'Wouldn't it?' she whispered.

He shook his head. 'I was no good for Laura—I'm no use for any woman—and I couldn't...I just couldn't bear it if I made you unhappy.'

'I don't think you'd make me unhappy, Robert,' she said huskily. 'In fact, I know you wouldn't, and I'm going to say the words whether you want me to or not. I love you, Robert Cunningham.'

He didn't answer, and it was she who took a step towards him, hesitantly, uncertainly, and for a second she thought he was going to back away, then suddenly his face cracked.

'Oh, hell! Oh, hell, Hannah!'

And suddenly she was in his arms, and he was covering her face with tiny, searing kisses and brokenly saying her name over and over again. Tears slid from the corner of her eyes as his lips claimed hers, his mouth hungry, desperate, and she kissed him back just as fervently, giving him all that she was, knowing only that this was right. This was meant to be.

'You're beautiful...so beautiful,' he murmured into her throat, his breathing shallow and unsteady as he carried her into the bedroom, then gently removed her clothes, leaving her dressed only in her bra and briefs.

'I'm not,' she mumbled, suddenly awkward and embarrassed as his gaze travelled over her. 'I'm too skinny.'

Gently he reached out and cupped her lace-covered breasts in his hands. Even more gently he caressed each one through the fabric with his thumb until her already tingling nipples hardened with a pleasure that was almost pain. 'Hannah, you're so beautiful I want to throw you on that bed and make love to you until dawn, but...'

'But?' she gasped, her eyes large and luminous, her breathing now as unsteady as his.

'Are you absolutely sure you want to do this?' His hands slid down her sides and came to rest on the waistband of her briefs. 'Please...please, be sure, because this time...this time even if St Stephen's itself burst into flames, I wouldn't be able to stop.'

'I don't want you to stop,' she said, putting her hands over his and gently pushing downwards so her briefs slipped to the floor. 'And believe me,' she added, unclipping her bra so her breasts sprang free. 'Believe me, I have never been more sure of anything in my life.'

And she *was* sure as he gathered her to him. Was never more certain as he paid tender homage to every inch of her throbbing body with his mouth and hands and tongue. And when he finally joined with her, and took her to heights she'd never even dreamt of, far less imagined, she knew that this was the man she'd been born for.

CHAPTER NINE

'YOU'RE not actually going to eat all of that, are you?' Elliot exclaimed, cradling a cup of black coffee in his hands and gazing with a barely concealed shudder at Hannah's canteen dinner of chicken pie, chips and beans.

'You bet I am,' she said with a grin, forking a piece of pie into her mouth to prove it. 'In fact, I have it on the very highest authority that nobody should start a shift in A and E without a decent meal inside them.'

'Uh-huh. And this highest authority...' Elliot took a sip of coffee and cocked his head at her thoughtfully. 'He wouldn't happen to be a tall, dark-haired individual who goes by the name of Robert Edward Cunningham, would he?'

Hannah's lips quirked. 'Maybe.'

'Uh-*huh*. And as I appear to be on a winning roll here, would I also be right in surmising that this particular Robert Edward Cunningham and a certain Dr Hannah Blake have finally got it together?'

'Elliot—'

'Because if they haven't,' he continued doggedly as a rosy glow crept across her cheeks, 'I want to know why Robert's been going around A and E for the last three weeks with a silly grin on his face, and you have the look of a girl who has been very soundly loved.'

Hannah blushed scarlet, but with over sixty members of staff eating and talking in the canteen this evening she reckoned she could probably have shrieked 'Stop, thief!' and no one would have heard her. 'OK, all right. We're sort of together—'

151

'About damn time.'

'But we don't want anybody to know about it yet,' she insisted. 'It's too soon, you see.'

He drew a finger across his throat. 'Not a word will pass my lips, love. All I want to know is whether you're happy.'

She was. Blissfully, unbelievably happy. And no more so than when she was bidding a decorous goodnight to Robert in the staffroom—a goodnight he always echoed just as solemnly—and knew that within half an hour she'd be in his flat, in his bed, and they would be making glorious, unending love until the sun rose.

'You're the best thing that's ever come into my life,' Robert had murmured into her hair one morning as he'd held her close. 'But Laura and I... We didn't really know one another before we got married, and this time I don't want any secrets between us—no dark corners—so neither of us will ever have any regrets.'

Regrets—how could she possibly have any regrets? she wondered. She loved him, and knew he loved her. OK, so maybe he hadn't actually said that he did, but Laura had hurt him badly and it would take time for him to trust her. Time for him to realise she truly did love him, and they had all the time in the world for him to learn that.

'Have you told him who your father is yet?' Elliot asked abruptly.

Well, perhaps not all the time, she realised, putting down her knife and fork, her appetite suddenly gone.

'Almost.'

'Hannah, you can't "almost" tell someone something like that,' Elliot protested. 'Either you have, or you haven't!'

She bit her lip. 'Look, I'll get round to it, OK? It's been a bit difficult, finding the right moment—'

'Good grief, woman, how can there possibly be a wrong

moment? All you have to do is open your mouth and say, "Charles Blake is my father."'

'Yes, but—'

'Sweetheart, you *have* to tell him. Believe me, the longer you wait, the harder it will get, and if Robert finds out himself...' He rolled his eyes heavenwards. 'Hannah, I don't have half the hang-ups that Robert Cunningham does, but if I was in love with you, and you kept something like this a secret from me, even I'd start to wonder what else you had to hide. Love, you've *got* to tell him—and tell him soon.'

'I will—I promise I will,' she insisted. 'When...when the time is right.'

And as Elliot shook his head and swore under his breath, neither of them noticed that Jerry Clark was sitting two tables from them, a thoughtful, malicious smile spreading across his face.

'Ten years ago A and E would have been packed to the rafters on November 5th with burns cases like this,' Robert murmured as he and Hannah carefully began covering the burns on Harry Ryan's hands and arms with sterile, non-stick, moist dressings. 'This poor little chap's our first casualty, and hopefully he's going to be our last.'

'That advertising campaign the government did a few years back certainly made a huge difference,' Hannah observed, as the whooshes and bangs in the distance indicated that somewhere in the city yet another bonfire-night display was getting under way. 'When the public saw the kinds of horrific injuries both adults and children could get from exploding fireworks, most people decided to take their kids to organised events instead of having parties in their back gardens.'

'It's a pity Harry's parents didn't do that.' Robert sighed. 'Imagine anyone being stupid enough to allow a six-year-old to hold a box of fireworks. You wonder where some people's brains are.' He glanced across at Jane. 'How's his BP and pulse rate now?'

'Stabilising nicely now the IVs are up and running,' she replied.

Robert nodded. The biggest danger in a case like this—apart from the severity of the burns—was that the victim would go into hypovolaemic shock when the body attempted to repair itself by withdrawing fluids from the uninjured areas of the body. Replacing those lost fluids as quickly as possible was imperative before liver and kidney damage could occur.

'What should we do about the minor blisters on the side of his neck?' Hannah asked, smiling encouragingly down at the little boy who was lying, white-faced and tearstained, on the trolley, a nasal cannula plugged into his nose to give him added oxygen. 'Should we dress them as well, or—?'

'Leave them alone,' Robert said, staring at the blisters critically. 'The burns unit won't thank us for sending him up looking like a mummy, and they have their own procedures for dealing with minor injuries.'

'Then I think that's all we can do,' Hannah said, putting the last of the dressings in place and straightening up. 'Like you said, the rest is really up to the burns unit.'

And they'd have their work cut out with this one, she thought sadly as Harry Ryan was wheeled out of the treatment room. He'd sustained third-degree burns to his hands and arms and it was going to take years of painful skin grafts to repair the damage. And even then there would be no guarantee that he'd ever fully regain the use of his hands and arms.

'Our burns unit is one of the best in London, Hannah,' Robert murmured, clearly reading her mind.

'I know,' she replied. 'It's just... He's so very little Robert, and I keep thinking if he were mine...'

'If he was yours, I'm sure you'd have taken much better care of him so he didn't end up here in the first place,' Robert declared firmly.

She was tempted to tell him that hundreds of children with good and caring parents ended up in hospital every day. That she'd met some children in the short time she'd worked in A and E who seemed to have been born with a suicide mission in life, but she didn't.

She was too busy suddenly wondering what it would be like to have a child of her own. She'd never thought of herself as a mother, never even imagined herself as one, but now… To feel a child growing inside her, to watch its first tottering steps. And she didn't want just anybody's child, she realised. She wanted Robert Cunningham's.

'Maybe…maybe one day, Hannah?' he said softly, glancing down at her with a knowing smile.

'I'd like that,' she replied, her own lips creasing in response. 'I'd like that very much indeed.'

'And I'm sure whatever it is you'd both like is really interesting, but we do have patients waiting,' Mr Mackay observed tersely as he strode past them.

Robert stared after the A and E consultant, open-mouthed, then grinned. 'That is the first time in my life I've actually been accused of wasting time. What are you doing to me, Hannah Blake?'

'Making you a little more human, I hope.' She chuckled, but as he walked away she noticed Jane looking at her from across the treatment room, a puzzled, quizzical look on her face.

It had been a look she'd seen before over the last three weeks. A look that made her wonder how much longer she and Robert would be able to keep their relationship a secret. Frankly, she was amazed they'd managed it this long. Sometimes she thought it must be obvious to everyone. And sometimes, when Robert smiled at her—that very special smile she knew he reserved solely for her—she was certain the whole world must know.

'I take my hat off to you, Hannah.'

'You do?' she replied, whirling round guiltily to see Floella behind her. 'Why—what have I done?'

'Only single-handedly managed to turn our special registrar from the grouch of the millennium into a big, cuddly pussy cat.' The staff nurse beamed. 'I don't know what you said to him a couple of weeks ago but he's been a different man ever since. In fact, I actually heard him *whistling* when he came on duty tonight.'

He whistled in the bath every morning, too. Well, he hadn't this morning, but that could have had something to do with the fact that she'd joined him, and he'd had other things on his mind at the time.

'You OK, Hannah?' Floella continued with a slight frown. 'You look a bit flushed. Liz in Admin was telling me there's a flu bug going round the hospital—'

'I'm not surprised, considering they keep the temperature in here on a level with Barbados while outside it's freezing,' Hannah declared quickly. 'It's enough to make anybody sick. And talking about sick, who's next?'

'Ben Ryder—three years old—sounds like asthma.'

It wasn't. In fact, by the time she'd finished examining the little boy she was completely stumped.

'You said your son only started wheezing recently, Mrs Ryder?' she queried as she put down her stethoscope.

The small, dark-haired woman nodded. 'He was as right as rain at teatime, Doctor, or I'd never have taken him to the fireworks display, but when we got home he started to sound like this.'

'Has he ever shown any signs of bronchitis—asthma?' she asked, clutching at straws.

'No, never. In fact, he had his check-up at the clinic only last week, and they said he was as fit as a fiddle.'

Hannah's frown deepened. Ben Ryder's temperature, pulse and blood pressure were normal. There were no signs of blueness about his lips or tongue, and he was alert, if a little tearful.

In fact, if he hadn't got this wheeze—a wheeze that seemed to be getting worse—she would have said there was nothing wrong with the child. Perhaps she should page Paediatrics, get their consultant to come down and have a look. Ben could have a lung or a heart problem that hadn't been detected yet. Or maybe he was suffering from a severe allergic reaction to something, and his wheezing was the precursor to him going into full anaphylactic shock.

And, then again, perhaps not. An idea suddenly flashed into her mind.

'Jane, would you tilt Ben's head for me?'

Quickly the sister did as she asked.

'Can you see anything? Mrs Ryder whispered as Hannah squinted up into the little boy's nose.

A donkey, Hannah thought with a smile, remembering Robert's words. It was a donkey, not a zebra.

'Your son's got a stone up his nose, Mrs Ryder,' she announced as she straightened up. 'While you were watching the fireworks he must have got a bit bored, picked one up and stuck it up his nose.'

'Why, the little…' Mrs Ryder was torn between laughter, exasperation and tears. 'Can you get it out?'

'Jane, could you get me the smallest forceps you can find, please?' Hannah asked.

Within seconds the stone was out, and Mrs Ryder was carrying a thoroughly chastened Ben out of the treatment room.

'Take a tip from me, Doctor,' Mrs Ryder said wryly. 'Don't ever have children. Not only do they give you grey hairs, the only way a woman can survive is to grow eyes in the back of her head!'

Hannah laughed, but her face became slightly pensive when the mother and son had gone. Grey hairs and eyes in the back of her head seemed a small price to pay to have a miniaturised version of Robert. A tiny, black-haired, grey-eyed bundle of mischief who would stick stones up his nose and get into all kinds of scrapes. Or perhaps even a daughter who would have Robert's black hair and smile, and…

For goodness' sake, get a grip! her mind shrieked. The man hasn't even told you he loves you yet, and you're already thinking children, a future, a lifetime together.

Because this is right, her heart answered back. Because even when I was engaged to Chris, I never thought of myself with children of my own, never really thought beyond the wedding day, but with Robert…

With Robert she could picture the two of them growing old together, worrying about their children together, and still loving and caring for one another.

'You wouldn't credit the things children can get up to when you take your eyes off them for a second, would you?' Jane chuckled.

Hannah shook her head and smiled. 'Have you ever thought about having children, Jane?' she asked before she could stop herself.

'Have I ever…?' The sister looked at her in surprise. 'What on earth put that question into your head?'

'I don't know,' Hannah replied, all too annoyingly aware that she was blushing. 'Maybe I'm getting broody or something.'

'I'd watch it, then,' Jane chuckled again. 'Quite normal, rational women have been known to get themselves into all sorts of trouble when they start to get broody.'

'I'll remember that,' Hannah said, fighting down her mounting colour without success. 'But, seriously, Jane, *have* you ever thought about having children?'

The sister sighed, her grey eyes suddenly a little rueful,

almost a little sad. 'Of course I have, but some things…some things just aren't meant to be. You can love someone until you're blue in the face, and if they don't even know you're around…'

Jane wasn't looking at her as she spoke but at something else across the room, and as Hannah followed her gaze she suddenly realised with a shock that it wasn't a something the sister was gazing at so wistfully, but a someone.

Elliot Mathieson.

Sensible, level-headed Sister Halden was in love with Elliot Mathieson. She would never have guessed it—not in a million years.

'Jane—'

'Did I tell you that bloke with the steel bar in his chest is doing really well in Intensive Care?' her colleague interrupted. 'The newspapers are calling him the miracle man, and I'm not surprised. Just the thought of having a steel bar imbedded in my chest is enough to give me nightmares.'

It wasn't a very subtle way of changing the subject—in fact, it wasn't subtle at all—but what could Hannah say? That she was sure everything would turn out right for Jane in the end? They both knew it wouldn't. They both knew only too well that Elliot was never going to settle down with anyone.

'Jane, I'm sorry—'

'Lord, but standing here talking about children isn't getting on with the work.' The girl smiled with an effort. 'I've a stack of forms to fill in and if I don't get them in before Friday Admin will hang me out to dry and I won't be a sister any more, far less a mother!'

Hannah chuckled but her laughter died when Jane bustled off purposefully down the treatment room.

To love someone, and know they scarcely noticed you… She'd experienced a little of that with Robert, and it had been miserable, wretched. She was so lucky, she thought as she checked the white board, then walked quickly towards cubicle 1. Lucky that the man she'd fallen in love with loved her. Lucky that for once in her life everything seemed to be going right.

In fact, she felt so happy today that she didn't even feel angry when the patient asked for a second opinion. All she felt was irritated.

'It sounds to me from his symptoms that he's got a classic case of heartburn,' Robert declared when she explained her problem. 'To be fair to your patient, it can be very easy to think you're having a heart attack if the pain is really severe, but if you were having a heart attack the pain wouldn't be worse at night when you lie down, then get better when you sit up.'

'*I* know that—and *you* know that,' she said, 'but I just can't convince *him*. I've shown him his ECG reading—even let him see his BP—but the trouble is that his father died at forty-two from a cardiac arrest and he's convinced the same thing's going to happen to him.'

'Cubicle 1, you said?' Robert queried. 'OK. Leave him to me.'

And to her amazement, within fifteen minutes Robert was escorting a clearly very relieved patient towards the exit.

'How did you do that—what did you say?' she demanded.

'Trade secret.' He grinned.

'You're not getting away with that,' she protested. 'Come on—confession time.'

He laughed. 'OK. I simply gave him some hospital-strength indigestion-busting solution which eased his heartburn, and when the pain disappeared he had to accept he wasn't dying after all.'

'Robert Cunningham, you're wonderful!' Hannah beamed.

He glanced over his shoulder, then back at her, and his voice when he spoke was husky. 'And have I told you recently that I think you're pretty wonderful, too?'

A smile curved her lips. 'Oh, maybe once or twice.'

'Once or twice?' he protested.

'OK, make that three or four times.' She laughed, her eyes sparkling.

He stared at her for a moment, indignation and amusement warring with each other on his face, then growled, 'Woman, will you stop looking at me like that?'

'Like what?' she protested, truly bewildered.

'All flushed, and glowing, and completely and utterly desirable.' Robert shook his head ruefully. 'Hannah, you're playing hell with my concentration. All I can think when I look at you is roll on half past eleven.'

'Something special happening at half past eleven, is there?' she asked, schooling her features into a picture of bland innocence.

'I'm hoping so,' he replied, his eyes suddenly gleaming. 'I'm hoping that by the time I get back to Wellington Place a very special girl might be waiting in my bed for me.'

'Well, I suppose you can always hope,' she replied, deciding to tease him just a little, and saw a smile tug at the corners of his mouth.

'And if this very special, very particular girl *should* happen to be in my bed,' he continued, his eyes fixed on her, dark with promise, 'and *should* happen to be willing...'

'Willing to do what?' she said a little breathlessly.

'Turn up at half past eleven, and you'll find out.' He winked.

A splutter of laughter came from her as he disappeared into his office, laughter that became acute consternation when she noticed Floella and Jane tucking into a huge box of chocolates.

'Oh, heck, it's not somebody's birthday today, is it, and I've forgotten?' she asked as she joined them.

'Uh-uh,' Floella mumbled through a mouthful of chocolate. 'Do you remember Sheila Vernon?'

Hannah frowned. 'Can't say the name rings a bell.'

'Of course it does,' the staff nurse protested. 'Ruptured ovarian cyst. The gynae consultant came down to confirm it, and he wasn't best pleased at the time because he'd been having coffee with Gussie Granton up in Paediatrics. That's all off, by the way,' Floella continued, helping herself to another chocolate. 'Gorgeous Gussie's on the loose again, and rumour has it that as Elliot and Robert are the only male members of staff she hasn't dated—'

'You were talking about Sheila Vernon, Flo?' Hannah said pointedly.

'Were we?' The staff nurse frowned. 'Oh—yes, so we were. Well, apparently she was discharged from Women's Surgical last week, and in grateful thanks for the care she got at St Stephen's she sent a box of chocs to Women's Surgical and one to us.'

'How very kind of her,' Hannah exclaimed, popping a chocolate into her mouth.

'Unusual, too,' Jane observed. 'Most people remember to thank the staff on the wards after they've come in as an emergency, but precious few remember the poor Cinderellas down in The Pit who first diagnosed what was wrong with them. In fact, I can remember one time when—'

'Hannah, could I have a word with you?' Robert interrupted, appearing beside them without warning.

'Would you like a chocolate?' She smiled, holding the box out to him. 'Sheila Vernon—'

'No, I don't want a chocolate. What I want is a word with you—*now*!'

Slowly she put the box of chocolates down. Something was wrong—very badly wrong. His face was white and taut, and mentally she reviewed all the casualties she'd seen that night. There'd been nothing particularly serious—actually, it had been a relatively quiet evening for them, apart from the constant sounds of rockets and bangers going off outside the hospital.

'Robert—'

'In my office!'

He whirled round on his heel before she could say another word, and quickly she followed him, all too aware that Floella and Jane were staring after her with concern. His office. Not the staffroom for a cup of coffee and a cosy chat. His office meant he didn't want anyone to hear their conversation. His office meant trouble—big trouble.

'What is it—what's wrong?' she asked, the moment he'd shut the door.

'This!' he exclaimed, picking up a sheet of paper from his desk and waving it under her nose. 'I want to know if what it says in this is true!'

'If you'd keep the damn thing still long enough for me to be able to read it, I might be able to answer you,' Hannah said, bewildered. 'What is it?'

'I came in to collect some files I needed and found this anonymous note on my desk.'

'Bin it,' she declared firmly. 'Anybody who hasn't got the guts to sign their name—'

'Is Charles Blake your father?'

The colour drained from her face instantly. Never in all her wildest dreams would she have imagined that he might want to speak to her about that. 'Robert—'

'Is—it—true?' he said, each word cold and clipped.

She stared at him unhappily for a second, then nodded. 'Yes—yes, it's true, but, Robert, I can explain…'

Furiously he threw the sheet of paper down on his desk, and distractedly she noticed it was typed. She supposed people who wrote anonymous letters always typed their poison, and seeing Robert's face—his eyes a mixture of anger, hurt and disillusionment—she knew that if she ever found out who'd sent it, she'd pummel them senseless.

'Robert…' She put her hand out to him and felt utter dismay when he backed away. 'Robert, does it matter who my father is?'

'Yes, yes, it matters,' he said, his lips compressed into a tight white line. 'It matters because you didn't tell me. It matters because I had to find out from…from this…' He picked up the sheet of paper again and crushed it between his fingers. 'And it matters because you *lied* to me.'

'I didn't lie! I just…' She flushed scarlet. 'I just didn't tell you.'

'And why not, Hannah? Why didn't you tell me?'

'I didn't think it was important,' she faltered. 'Elliot said I should—'

'You told Elliot?' he thundered, and she flinched. 'Who else at St Stephen's knows? The porters, the cleaners, the guy who sells newspapers in the canteen?'

'Only our consultant,' she said quickly, 'and he only knows because it's on my CV, but I didn't tell Elliot—he found out himself.'

'And that's supposed to make me feel better, is it?' He strode over to his waste-paper bin and threw in the letter. 'That's supposed to make everything all right?'

She took a hesitant step towards him. 'Robert, when I came to St Stephen's I didn't want anyone to know who my father is because I didn't want anybody to have any preconceptions about me. I wanted to be judged on my own merits—'

'Yeah, right.'

'I did!' she insisted as his lip curled. 'My father didn't even know where I was working—I wouldn't tell him—'

'Because you knew he'd think you were slumming it with the peasants in St Stephen's?'

She stiffened. 'I don't know who you're insulting most by saying that—me, or everyone else who works here.'

He had the grace to flush slightly, but he wasn't finished, not by a long shot.

'I'm surprised *Daddy* didn't offer to get you a post in some nice, comfortable, civilised, private hospital.'

'I didn't want a job like that.' Oh, hell, that hadn't come out at all the way she'd intended, she realised, seeing his eyebrows snap down. 'I mean—I meant—I wanted to get a post on my own without his help. I didn't tell him I'd got a job here—I don't know how he found out—'

'That letter I brought round to your flat,' Robert interrupted with dawning comprehension. 'It was from him, wasn't it?'

She nodded. 'And if you think back, you might remember I wasn't exactly over the moon to receive it. Robert...Robert, surely all that really matters here is you and me, not who my father is?'

For a second she felt she'd almost convinced him, then he shook his head.

'If your father had been a teacher or a dustman, it wouldn't have mattered a brass farthing to me, but your father is Charles Blake, Hannah, one of the foremost consultants in the country.'

'Yes, but—'

'And the only reason I can come up with to explain your reluctance to say anything is that you're ashamed of your association with me. You thought I might want to meet him, and you didn't want to introduce somebody ordinary and run-of-the-mill like me to your precious father.'

Of course she wasn't ashamed of him—she'd never be ashamed of him—but he was right, she suddenly realised with dismay. She hadn't wanted him to meet her father.

Time and time again she'd put it off, convincing herself that now wasn't the right moment, that tomorrow would be better, but the bottom line was that she hadn't told him because she'd been afraid. Afraid that once Robert knew, he might become like Chris. Afraid he might become so obsessed with what her father could do for him that she'd be sidelined, marginalised into a small corner of his life.

It was an ignoble thought—an unworthy one. She knew Robert was nothing like Chris, would never be anything like Chris, but the tiny seed of doubt had been there. The tiny gnawing seed of doubt had kept her silent.

And Robert saw the shame in her face and misinterpreted it completely.

'So, I was right!' he exclaimed, a tide of dark, livid colour appearing on his cheekbones. 'You *are* ashamed of me. I'm just some bit of rough you've picked up for convenient sex until Daddy selects someone more suitable for you to settle down with and raise 2.2 children!'

'No—*No*!' she gasped in horror. 'Robert, I *love* you!'

'Love means trust, Hannah,' he said tightly. 'Love means honesty. If I learned nothing else when I was married to Laura, I learned that.'

He was already walking to his office door, and she hurried after him.

'OK...OK, you want honesty from me—I'll give you honesty,' she said. 'I didn't tell you who my father was because...because I was frightened.'

He turned to face her, his eyes cold, impassive. 'Frightened of what?'

'Robert, all my life I've known—been told—how brilliant my father is, how talented. All my life I've known that as soon as I've said I'm his daughter, all anybody wanted to talk about was him.'

'Go on.'

Never had he looked so grim, so unapproachable, but she'd started and she knew she couldn't stop now.

'I fell in love two years ago—or rather I thought I did. His name was Chris, and we were going to be married until I found out he only wanted to marry me because he hoped my father would help his career.'

'And you thought I might be the same?' he exclaimed, anger and hurt plain in his eyes. 'You thought I was a scumbag like that?'

'No—*no*!' Oh, she was saying this all wrong. Her words were coming out all tangled and twisted and wrong. 'No, I didn't think that—I know I didn't—but I think that perhaps…perhaps…'

'You're saying you didn't trust me. That's what you're saying, isn't it?' he demanded.

She gazed pleadingly up at him, willing him to understand. 'I wanted to trust you. I was sure that I did, but… Robert, you can have no idea what it's like to grow up knowing no one's interested in you, only your father. To stand in your own home when your father gives a dinner party and pray—*pray*—that somebody might talk to you because you're you, and not because you're Charles Blake's daughter.'

He stared at her for a long moment, then his lip curled. 'You're right, Hannah, I don't understand. You see, my family were too dirt poor to give any kind of party, far less a dinner party.'

'Robert—'

'We have patients waiting, Dr Blake. They require our medical skills, and I suggest we get back to them.'

'But, Robert, we haven't finished—'

'Oh, but we have,' he said, his face a cold mask. 'We have most certainly, definitely finished.'

And before she could utter a word he'd gone, leaving her standing in the centre of the empty office, knowing that it wasn't just their conversation that was finished. They were, too.

CHAPTER TEN

'THANK God you've made it in this morning, Hannah!' Jane exclaimed with relief, when she came through the treatment-room doors. 'Honestly, I don't know if I'm on my head or my heels today. What with half the hospital staff down with flu, and the other half marooned at home because of this snow...'

'And Maintenance say it's getting worse,' Kelly Ross chipped in as she joined them. 'Apparently there's almost six inches of snow on the pavements now, and there's no sign of it stopping.'

'Oh, terrific,' Jane groaned. 'The next thing you know we'll be—'

'Jane, could you make sure Admin gets those requisition forms today?' Robert interrupted. 'They've been on the phone, saying they should have received them yesterday, and I've promised you'll fill them in and send them along.'

'Then you'll just have to phone them back and *un*promise,' the sister protested. 'Robert, you've seen what the waiting room's like. I'll be lucky if I get a chance to go to the loo, far less put pen to paper today.'

Irritation was plain on his face but he didn't say a word, and as he walked away a deep frown creased Jane's forehead.

'You know, this is going to sound really dumb and downright contrary of me,' she murmured, 'but I think I preferred it when he got angry. Oh, I don't mean I want him snippy and impatient all the time again, but...'

'It's like standing next to a rumbling volcano.' Kelly nodded. 'You don't know when it's going to explode, only

169

that it's going to, and the suspense is killing you. Hannah—'

'Sorry, but I have to go,' she said hurriedly. 'I think Flo wants me.'

And she did, judging by the staff nurse's wave, but Hannah would have grasped at any excuse to get away from what looked like developing into an in-depth discussion of what could possibly be wrong with Robert.

She didn't need a discussion. She knew what was wrong. He was angry with her. Angry, and hurt, and disappointed, but instead of exploding—getting his anger out into the open—he was turning it inwards, allowing it to simmer and fester, and as Kelly had said, one day it was going to blow.

'There wasn't any need for you to rush,' Floella remarked with a smile. 'It's no big emergency, just a tourist from the States who suffers from high blood pressure and has lost his medication. He's not registered in this country with a GP, so—'

'He's hoping we can provide a prescription for the drugs he needs,' Hannah finished for her. 'OK, I'll have a word with him. What's his name?'

Floella's lips twitched. 'Would you believe Rock Cadwallader?'

He didn't look like a Cadwallader in his denim jeans, cowboy boots and a jacket that wouldn't have looked out of place in the Rocky Mountains. But as the American got to his feet, and Hannah stared up at what must have been six feet five inches of solid muscle, she decided he most definitely looked like a rock.

'It's the most vexatious thing, ma'am,' he declared in answer to her query. 'I always keep the dang pills with me, never pack them in my luggage, but when I checked into the hotel, the little critters had disappeared. I reckon I must have pulled them out of my pocket when I was consulting my little old *London A-Z* street atlas.'

Good grief. He only had to add 'Aw shucks' and 'heavens to Betsy', and she'd be wondering where he'd parked his horse, Hannah thought, suppressing a smile as she took his blood pressure.

'Gone right through the roof, has it?' he asked when she straightened up with a slight frown.

'It's certainly higher than it should be,' she admitted, 'but I shouldn't think the worry over losing your medication has done it a lot of good. Can you remember what your doctor prescribed for you?'

'Not the brand names, I'm afraid, but I can give you my doc's address and telephone number, and he'll be able to tell you. All I know is that I'm on beta blockers, ACE inhibitors and a vasodilator.'

'You must rattle,' Hannah said with a smile, and a broad grin lit up Mr Cadwallader's deeply tanned face.

'Sure do. In fact, my secretary reckons she can hear me three blocks away.'

Hannah laughed. 'Do you have your doctor's telephone number with you? Oh, terrific. I'll get our receptionist to telephone him, then you can be on your way.'

'Much obliged to you, ma'am,' he replied. 'I wouldn't want to be without my drugs for any length of time in this cold weather, and it's cold enough out there today to freeze the hide right off a skunk.'

Hannah didn't know if it would, but Reception had told her that they'd already been inundated by patients suffering from breathing problems because of the sub-zero temperature, not to mention the fractured limbs caused by people slipping on the snow-covered pavements and a rash of car accidents due to by the treacherous roads.

'Is that guy for real?' Elliot gasped, when Mr Cadwallader had gone, after kissing Hannah soundly on both cheeks and waving her a cheery farewell.

'You'd better believe it.' She chuckled. 'In fact, he's very big in ladies underwear in the States—'

'I'm surprised he can find anything to fit him—'

'And… *And*,' she continued with a reproving glance at Elliot, though her eyes sparkled, 'he's also promised to send me some extremely expensive briefs and bras when he gets home as a thank you for all my help.'

'Carried out a personal fitting, did he?' the SHO asked, his eyebrows waggling.

'Certainly not.' She laughed. 'I'll have you know that Mr Rock Cadwallader is a perfect gentleman.'

'Or a fool, like somebody else I could mention,' Elliot sighed as Robert strode past them with the barest of nods. 'How much longer is he going to keep this up, Hannah?'

'Permanently, I'm afraid,' she replied with a brave attempt at a smile that didn't fool Elliot for a second. 'You warned me this would happen so I really only have myself to blame.'

'Yes, but it's been over a month now,' the SHO protested. 'Have you tried talking to him again, explaining…'

'He thinks I was using him, Elliot,' she interrupted, a dull tide of colour spreading across her too-pale cheeks. 'It's not simply that I didn't tell him who my father was. He thinks I was only amusing myself with him until someone better came along.'

He stared at her in disbelief. 'But it's obvious you're in love with him. Good heavens, you light up like a neon sign whenever he's near.'

'If I do, then he either doesn't see it or doesn't choose to, which is why…why I've got myself another job. I had to, Elliot,' she continued as his jaw dropped. 'The atmosphere in A and E's impossible. Kelly said it was like working next to a rumbling volcano, and she's right, and it's all my fault. There's so much anger inside Robert, so much hurt and bitterness, and every time he sees me, it simply fuels those feelings.'

'But, Hannah—'

'Elliot, I've admitted I was wrong, I've told him I'm sorry, but I won't beg.' Her bottom lip trembled and she brought it back rigidly under control. 'Call it pride, call it whatever you like, but if he can't accept my apology—can't understand why I did what I did—then maybe…maybe I'm better off without him.'

'Oh, love…'

'Aren't you going to ask me about my new job?' she said, forcing a smile to her lips, unable to bear the sympathy in Elliot's eyes. 'For all you know I could have got myself a post with some mega-rich oil sheikh who's going to shower me with diamonds, and give me the kind of life you only ever see in the movies.'

'If he's in the market for a male doctor, can I have a job, too?' Elliot grinned, knowing full well what she was doing, and why. 'What is this new job, then—where is it?'

'Botswana. I've been accepted by Médicins Sans Frontières,' she continued as his eyebrows rose. 'I saw an advertisement in the paper, asking for applications from doctors and nurses, and I contacted them, and they've accepted me.'

'So when do you leave?'

'In a month. I really should give six weeks' notice but when I handed in my resignation this morning to Mr Mackay he said he'd sort it out with Admin.'

'But that means you'll be leaving right after Christmas,' Elliot protested. 'Some of the staff won't be back from their holidays and they'll miss your farewell do.'

'I'd much rather you didn't organise anything,' Hannah said quickly. 'I haven't been here any length of time.'

'Since when did a minor detail like that ever stand in the

way of a good night out?' Elliot laughed. 'And we can't possibly let you go without a party.'

But I don't want a party, Hannah thought miserably as the SHO completely ignored all her protestations and began rattling off possible venues and whether a buffet would be preferable to a sit-down meal. All I want is to slip quietly and unobtrusively away, and never see Robert Cunningham again.

No, she didn't really want that. She might be angry with him, and hurt at the way he'd effectively shut her out of his life for the past month, but she still loved him.

If only he'd talk to her. If they could just talk she was sure she could make him see that she really did love him, that her fears had been born out of insecurity, not a lack of trust.

But he wouldn't talk to her. Oh, he was polite and courteous enough when they were treating patients together, but the minute she tried to instigate any kind of conversation other than a medical one he became as remote and distant as a sphinx.

Which was why she was leaving. Leaving before she embarrassed both herself and him by making a pointless and stupid scene. Leaving because she knew that as far as Robert was concerned their relationship was irrevocably over, and to stay on here, feeling as she did, would be impossible.

'I wish you weren't going,' Elliot said sadly. 'We're going to miss you. *I'm* going to miss you.'

'Rubbish!' Hannah smiled. 'If my replacement turns out to be a twenty-four-year-old blonde with a 40DD bust, one glance at her and I guarantee you won't even remember my name!'

He laughed, too, but as she walked away the smile rapidly faded from his lips. It was a shame, a damn shame. Hannah was clearly deeply unhappy, and Robert... Robert was watching Hannah as she walked over to the white board and it was obvious he was also miserable. Well, it was time for some straight talking, Elliot decided grimly, and this morning he was just the man to do it.

'Something I can do for you?' Robert said as the SHO strode purposefully towards him.

'More like the other way round, actually,' he answered. 'I want to know what the hell you think you're doing?'

'Right now, listening to my SHO not making a whole lot of sense,' Robert replied smoothly.

'It's Hannah.'

'There's a problem with her work?'

'Of course there isn't a problem with her work,' Elliot protested, thrusting his hands through his blond hair with exasperation. 'Robert, you're in love with her, she's in love with you—'

'And I don't think my private life—or Dr Blake's for that matter—is any of your concern.'

'Dr Blake—*Dr Blake*. Dammit, Robert, this is Hannah we're talking about!' Elliot flared. 'She's the best thing that ever walked into your life, and she's going to walk right out again if you don't do something soon. Laura—'

'You can stop right there!' Robert interrupted, his face ice-cold.

'No, I damn well won't!' the SHO retorted. 'I never thought you and Laura were right for each other—'

'And since when did you become an expert on women?' Robert exclaimed, equally angry now. 'Married to Donna for three years, divorced for five, and all you've got to show for your thirty-two years is a string of girlfriends, none of whom has lasted longer than a month!'

'Which is why when someone special like Hannah comes along a man should grab hold of her with both hands,' Elliot insisted. 'Robert, you love her. Don't drive her away because of a misplaced sense of pride. Hold onto her!'

Robert stared at him coldly, only the jerking of a muscle at the side of his jaw betraying just how very angry he was. 'Have you finished?'

'Robert, listen to me—'

'Butt out of my life, Elliot. Butt out, and if you've got any sense, keep out!'

The nerve of the man—the sheer, unmitigated gall— Robert thought furiously as he strode down the treatment room. Kelly took one look at his face and scuttled quickly out of his path.

Just who did Elliot think he was? Handing out advice like some third-rate, half-baked agony aunt. He didn't need any advice. He knew the score. Hannah hadn't trusted him, and she'd used him. That was it. End of story.

And do you truly believe she was using you? his mind demanded. Do you honestly think she's nothing more than a pampered rich kid who decided that some sex with a bit of rough would make her life at St Stephen's more bearable?

He groaned aloud as he forced himself to remember the nights he'd spent with her. Hannah didn't possess the experience or the guile to use anybody. Emotionally she'd still been a virgin when he'd first made love to her, and it had been a wonder and a joy for him to watch her blossom in his arms, to see her grow in confidence, to...

And he didn't want to remember any of this, he realised, clenching his hands into hard, tight fists. It didn't alter anything, it didn't change anything. OK, so maybe she hadn't been using him and, OK, so she had a huge inferiority complex because of her father and what had happened with this Chris—damn him for all eternity—but nothing could excuse or alter the fact that she'd lied to him, deceived him. Dammit, he'd asked her for honesty, and if she couldn't even be honest about who her father was, there was no future for them.

'That man's going to burst a blood vessel if he doesn't get rid of what's eating him soon,' Floella observed as she watched Robert disappear into cubicle 8.

'We have patients to attend to, Flo,' Hannah said brusquely. 'And I'm sure Dr Cunningham is both big enough and old enough to sort out his own problems.'

'Yeah, right.' The staff nurse nodded, but as they walked together towards cubicle 2 Hannah couldn't help noticing that Flo was shooting her a very puzzled, thoughtful glance.

And to her dismay it was a glance Jane began to mirror as the rest of their shift sped by in an exhausting round of even more broken limbs, angina attacks and minor road accidents. Jane and Flo had clearly found time to put their heads together, and this time they'd come up with the correct answer.

Oh, how she wished it was already the end of December, she sighed wearily when her shift finally ended and she went along to the staffroom to collect her coat and handbag. Actually, make that January 1st, she amended with a sinking heart as she opened the staffroom door and found Robert waiting for her, his face a mixture of anger and bewilderment.

'Mr Mackay's just told me you've handed in your resignation, that you've taken a post with Médicins Sans Frontières?' he announced without preamble.

'That's right,' Hannah replied, amazed at how calm her voice sounded when she felt anything but.

'Are you out of your mind?' he protested. 'Hannah, doctors who work for Médicins Sans Frontières go into war zones, famine and flood areas!'

'There'd hardly be any point in setting up an organisation to help the victims of such catastrophes if the doctors they employed never travelled any further than Watford Gap, would there?' she pointed out, opening the door of her locker only to see him bang it shut.

'Hannah, you could get killed—you could catch any number of life-threatening diseases!'

'They're going to give me shots for typhus and cholera—'

'I don't give a damn if they inoculate you against every communicable disease known to mankind, you can't possibly do it!'

'You mean you don't think a pampered rich kid like me will be able to hack it?' she said tightly, opening her locker again and taking out her coat.

'I never said you were a pampered rich kid.'

'No, but you thought it, didn't you?' she retorted, and saw a betraying flush of colour darken his cheeks. 'And you're right—I was pampered as a child. So pampered that my father gave over the whole top of our house to me and my nanny when I was born, with a separate entrance and exit so that he wouldn't be disturbed by my presence. So pampered that I was able to keep a special calendar of the days when I actually saw him, when he remembered to talk to me.'

He stared at her, horrified. 'Hannah—'

'And I became even more pampered when I grew up,' she continued bitterly. 'He didn't send me away to boarding school as he could have done. Oh, no. He kept me home so that whenever I was lucky enough to see him he could ask how I'd got on at school, dissect my exam results and tell me how he'd always wanted a brilliant, talented son to follow in his footsteps and how disappointed he was to have fathered a dumb-cluck daughter instead.'

Robert was appalled. Appalled and furious, fit to kill. How could anyone treat another human being—let alone their own flesh and blood—like that? How could anyone be so self-absorbed that the feelings of their own child meant nothing to them?

'Hannah, I'm so sorry—'

'It's in the past now,' she said dismissively. 'I haven't seen my father in over two years, and I don't intend to. I have my own life to live, and that's what I mean to do.'

He stared down at his hands, then up at her. 'Hannah, this job you've accepted… Are you sure it's what you want?'

'It will be challenging, and I think that's what I need right now,' she replied slipping on her coat.

'Working at St Stephen's is a challenge,' he pointed out. 'Dealing with the constant stream of people who come through our doors is a challenge. Hannah, you're an excellent doctor, you fit in well with the team, you're a natural for A and E—'

'And with a glowing testimonial like that I could get a job in any A and E department in the country,' she interrupted. 'So why should I stay at St Stephen's?'

His gaze locked with hers for a second, then fled. 'Hannah… Hannah, you must know how I feel about you.'

'Must I?' she said, her heart suddenly beginning to race.

'Dammit, you should!' he flared. 'We were lovers in case you've forgotten. You're important to me, and I…I care about what happens to you.'

She was important to him. He cared about what happened to her. Perhaps a month ago that would have been enough. Perhaps a month ago she would have fallen happily into his arms again, and into his bed, but it wasn't enough any more. She wanted more. She wanted him to tell her he loved her.

'How much do you care, Robert?' she said through a throat so tight it hurt.

Say it, damn you, she thought as he stared down at her, his face unreadable. If you'd only say those three little words I'd phone the headquarters of Médicins Sans Frontières right now and ask them if I could possibly withdraw my acceptance.

But he didn't say them. He merely muttered, 'I have no right to try to run your life for you, Hannah, and if this is what you truly want…'

I want you, you big, stubborn idiot, she longed to yell back at him, but she didn't. Instead she quickly walked towards the staffroom door. 'I'll see you tomorrow, Robert.'

She half thought he would try to stop her. She definitely thought he might come after her, but he did neither, and tears welled in her eyes as she walked along to the waiting room.

Look, does it really matter if he doesn't say the words? her mind whispered. You know deep down that he really loves you. But it does matter, her heart answered back. If Robert can't say 'I love you' then maybe she'd been right when she'd told Elliot she'd be better off without him.

'I'm afraid it seems to be getting worse out there, Hannah,' one of the secretaries on Reception called as she passed. 'Would you like me to call you a taxi?'

'I'll be fine.' She managed to smile back. 'It's not as though I have very far to go.'

At least not yet, she thought when she stood outside the hospital and quickly unfurled her umbrella, but in a month's time…

In a month's time all this would be a distant memory. St Stephen's, the A and E department, all the staff who worked in it. And Robert. Would he become a distant memory, too?

No, he would never be that, she realised. She would always love him, always want him, and because her eyes were blurred with a mixture of tears and snow as she began crossing the road, and because her head was bent against the icy wind, she didn't see the car coming round the corner until it was too late. Didn't hear the screech of its brakes until it hit her, and then all she felt was a searing, agonising pain in her leg as she was dragged along the road.

Faintly she heard the sound of a car door opening, then a man hoarsely repeating that it hadn't been his fault, that she'd simply stepped out in front of him, but when she tried to raise her head, to tell the frightened voice that she was perfectly all right, hands began to lift her. Hands that belonged to worried faces. Hands that were making the pain in her leg worse, much worse, and when she fainted for the first time in her life, her last thought was that at least it didn't hurt any more. Nothing hurt any more.

So she didn't see Elliot's shocked face as they carried her into A and E. Didn't feel Jane's hand gently lifting her wrist to take her pulse, her expression horrified, and didn't hear the deep, guttural cry Robert gave when he realised who it was.

'I think I should handle this one, don't you?' Elliot said, striding towards him to bar his way.

'Like hell you will,' Robert exclaimed. 'I'm the special registrar—'

'And this is personal for you. She's our colleague, our friend, but to you—'

'Elliot, if you don't get out of my way, I swear I'll knock you from here into the waiting room!' Robert exploded. 'Jane, I want an ECG, CBC, guiac and urine tests.'

'Chest, pelvis and leg X-rays?' the sister queried, quickly inserting an IV line into Hannah's arm, then linking her to the heart monitor.

'Everything. I want X-rays of everything.'

Jane glanced across at Elliot, her eyebrows raised, and he nodded. 'You heard what the man said. He wants X-rays of everything.'

'BP 130 over 90, pulse 80 beats a minute,' Floella announced.

'Pretty good for someone who's just been dragged along

the road by a car,' Elliot murmured, listening to Hannah's chest through his stethoscope. 'In fact, I think it looks a lot worse than it actually is.'

Robert hoped that it was. He prayed that it was.

She looked so fragile and white lying on the trolley, her only vestige of colour the trickle of blood running down onto her cheek from the graze on her temple. If he should lose her... Oh, God, if he should lose her the same way he'd lost Laura, he knew he wouldn't want to go on living.

'What idiot demanded X-rays of everything?' Craig Larkin protested as he came through the cubicle curtains. 'Radiology isn't some branch of your local photographer's, you know.'

'Craig...' Jane caught him by the arm, and nodded her head in the direction of the trolley.

He looked across, gasped out loud, then muttered tightly, 'Fine. Right. X-rays of everything.'

'Guiac and urine tests normal, Robert,' Floella declared. 'ECG a little fast but not worryingly so, CBC perfect.'

Which only left the X-rays, he thought, unclenching his fingers slightly. 'Jane, could you—?'

'Well, hello there, sleepyhead,' the sister said with a smile as Hannah's eyes suddenly fluttered open. 'Honestly, the things people will do to get a few weeks off work!'

'Robert...?' she said faintly, and he was at her side in an instant. 'The car driver. It wasn't his fault—'

'Never mind about that now,' he interrupted. 'How do you feel?'

She tried to move and decided that was a very bad idea. 'Like a herd of elephants have trampled over me, then returned for a repeat performance.'

'That bad, eh?' he said softly, smoothing her hair gently back from her forehead.

She nodded. 'And worse.'

'One fractured left leg, and absolutely no other damage

that I can see,' Craig declared, beaming at her. 'Hannah Blake, I want you to know you've just taken ten years off my life.'

'Sorry,' she murmured, then winced.

'What is it—what's wrong?' Robert demanded. 'Have you a pain in your chest, difficulty in breathing?'

'No, I haven't got a pain in my chest, or difficulty in breathing,' she replied crossly, 'though I have to say it's a miracle that I don't, considering some idiot's got me wired up like a prize turkey!'

'I think we can safely say that Hannah's feeling better.' Elliot grinned, relief plain in his face.

She wasn't feeling better. Her leg hurt, her side hurt, and she felt a quite overwhelming desire to burst into tears, but she managed a wobbly smile. 'Please, won't somebody take all this paraphernalia off me? You heard what Craig said. I've just broken my leg.'

Elliot glanced enquiringly across at Robert and he nodded reluctantly, but when Jane and Floella had removed the ECG stickers, and Jane grasped the end of the trolley, ready to wheel Hannah to the plastering department, Elliot suddenly motioned to Robert to follow him.

'What's wrong?' Robert said as soon as they were standing outside the cubicle. 'Do you think we might have missed something?'

'No, of course I don't think we've missed something,' the SHO replied. 'I want to know when you're going to tell her.'

'Tell her what?' Robert said in confusion.

'That the local supermarket is doing a special this week on Christmas puddings!' Elliot exclaimed in exasperation. 'That you love her, of course, you idiot!'

'Elliot—'

'Robert, she could have been killed tonight, and then you'd never have had the chance. All you have to say is,

"I love you, Hannah." Why is that so very hard for you to say?'

'Elliot—'

'All that crap you gave Hannah about her not being honest with you. Have you been honest with her? *Have you?*'

He hadn't, Robert thought as the SHO hustled Floella and Jane out of the cubicle, muttering something garbled about needing to discuss something in private with them, then throwing him a meaningful look. He'd condemned Hannah for her failure to be honest with him, but he'd been anything but honest with her. All that rubbish about caring for her, about her being important to him. Damn it, he *loved* her, so why couldn't he just say it?

Because I'm afraid, he suddenly realised. I'm like Hannah, afraid to trust my own feelings. Afraid that, having made one mistake, I might be wrong again.

But he wasn't wrong this time, he knew he wasn't. He loved her, he always would, but after doubting her honesty, hurting her so badly, would she believe him?

There was only one way to find out.

'Where's everybody gone?' Hannah protested when he stepped back through the cubicle curtains. 'I was beginning to think I really did have something seriously wrong with me, and no one was willing to tell me.'

'You're fine, but I'm not,' he murmured, sitting down on the edge of the trolley and gently taking her hand in his. 'I've just found out I have an incurable affliction that only you can heal.'

'An incurable—'

'Hannah, when Laura died I swore I'd never fall in love again,' he continued as she gazed up at him in confusion. 'And then you came into my life. Little Miss Muffet, so eager and keen. Little Miss Muffet, with her big brown eyes and determination to put the world to rights.'

'Robert, I'm not Laura,' she began hesitantly. 'By all

accounts I don't have the figure, the height or the brains to be Laura even if I wanted to.'

'And I'm not Chris,' he said softly. 'I have neither the personal ambition nor the capacity to toady to anyone even if I wanted to.'

She stared down at the sheet covering her. 'I really do trust you, you know. I can see that it didn't look that way—'

'Hannah, I love you.'

'Y-you what?' she stammered.

'I love you, and I want to marry you.'

She gazed up at him in disbelief, then shook her head. 'I know what you're doing. You feel sorry for me because of this accident—'

'Hannah, I'm an A and E doctor,' he protested. 'If I proposed to every female accident victim I'd ever seen, I'd be a serial bigamist by now.'

'Yes, but—'

'Hannah, I *love* you. Do you want me to buy a mega-phone—stand outside the hospital and shout it to all of London? I'll do it if it will convince you. I love you, Hannah Blake, and I want to marry you, if you'll have me.'

'You mean it?' she whispered, her eyes fixed tremulously on his face. 'You're not simply saying it because I've been hurt? Robert—Robert, where are you going?' she added quickly as he got off the trolley and began to stride towards the cubicle curtains.

'To find a shop that sells megaphones! Hannah, I want you more than I've ever wanted anything in my life,' he declared as she began to laugh. 'So, will you marry me, have my children, grow old with me?'

She opened her mouth to tell him she'd like nothing better, only to gasp as she suddenly remembered some-thing. 'Robert, I'm supposed to be leaving for Botswana at the end of the month. I know I can't go now until my leg heals, but my contract's for two years. Once I leave Britain, I won't see you again for two years.'

'You will if Médicins Sans Frontières would be interested in employing a husband-and-wife team,' he said. 'One enthusiastic junior doctor married to a somewhat old and battered special registrar.'

'You'd do that for me?' she said huskily. 'Give up your career here at St Stephen's for me?'

He cupped her face gently in his hands. 'Hannah, don't you realise even now that you're more important to me than anything else in the world? I admit it will be a wrench to leave here. Elliot, Jane, Flo and myself, we've made a good team—but you and I could help so many people, working with Médicins Sans Frontières. People who desperately need us and our skills.'

'And we could come back,' she said thoughtfully. 'Once we'd fulfilled our contract, we could come back again and work here at St Stephen's, couldn't we?'

He nodded. 'So there really only appears to be one thing left that we haven't settled yet,' he murmured softly, placing tiny, feather-light kisses gently across her forehead 'For the *fourth* time, Hannah Blake, will you marry me?'

She gazed up at him, saw all the love and trust she had ever wanted to see in his face, and smiled. 'Oh, yes, Robert Oh, *yes*!'

And as his lips came down on hers, she thought she heard Elliot's delighted exclamation of 'About bloody time too!' coming from outside the cubicle, but all she really knew as Robert tenderly gathered her into his arms was that at last she had come home.

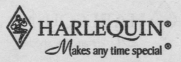

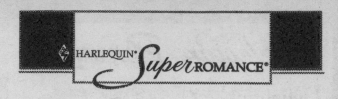

HARLEQUIN®
INTRIGUE
WE'LL LEAVE YOU BREATHLESS!

If you've been looking for thrilling tales of
contemporary passion and sensuous love stories
with taut, edge-of-the-seat suspense—then
you'll love Harlequin Intrigue!

Every month, you'll meet four new heroes
who are guaranteed to make your spine tingle
and your pulse pound. With them you'll enter
into the exciting world of Harlequin Intrigue—
where your life is on the line
and so is your heart!

THAT'S INTRIGUE—
ROMANTIC SUSPENSE
AT ITS BEST!

HARLEQUIN®
Makes any time special ®

Meet 50 loving dads in

babies
& BACHELORS USA

Take 4 FREE BOOKS,
Plus get a FREE GIFT!

Babies & Bachelors USA is a heartwarming new collection of reissued novels featuring 50 sexy heroes from every state who experience the ups and downs of fatherhood and find time for love all the same. All of the books, hand-picked by our editors, are outstanding romances by some of the world's bestselling authors, including Stella Bagwell, Kristine Rolofson, Judith Arnold and Marie Ferrarella!

Don't delay, order today! Call customer service at
1-800-873-8635.
Or
Clip this page and mail it to The Reader Service:

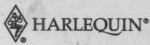